GHOST CANOE

1L

WILL HOBBS is the award-winning author of seven previous novels for young readers, including the Avon Camelot titles *Bearstone, Kokopelli's Flute,* and *Far North,* and the American Library Association has recognized four of Will's novels as Best Books for Young Adults. A graduate of Stanford University, Will lives in the mountains near Durango, Colorado, with his wife, Jean. In addition to their river and high country adventures in the Southwest, Will and Jean have been answering the call of the coast in recent years. The more they see of the Northwest, from Washington State to the island-studded Inside Passage of British Columbia and southeast Alaska, the more they find themselves returning. *Ghost Canoe*, Will's first mystery novel, is set on the very tip of Washington's Olympic Peninsula.

GHOST CANOE

WILL HOBBS

AN AVON CAMELOT BOOK

AVON BOOKS
A division of
The Hearst Corporation
1350 Avenue of the Americas
New York, New York 10019

First Avon Camelot Special Edition: January 1998
First Avon Camelot Printing: July 1998

CAMELOT TRADEMARK REG. U.S. PAT. OFF. AND IN OTHER COUNTRIES, MARCA REGISTRADA,
HECHO EN U.S.A.

Printed in the U.S.A.

OPM 10 9 8 7 6 5 4 3 2 1

*to John and Joyce Loftus
fellow travelers on this journey*

Strait of Juan de Fuca

Lighthouse   Tatoosh
              Island   Slant   Chibahdehl
                                         Rock   Rocks

Jones Rock   C A P E   F L A T T E R Y

                    Hole in
Fuca's   the Wall
Pillar

N.

Pacific
    Ocean   Makah
                                        Bay

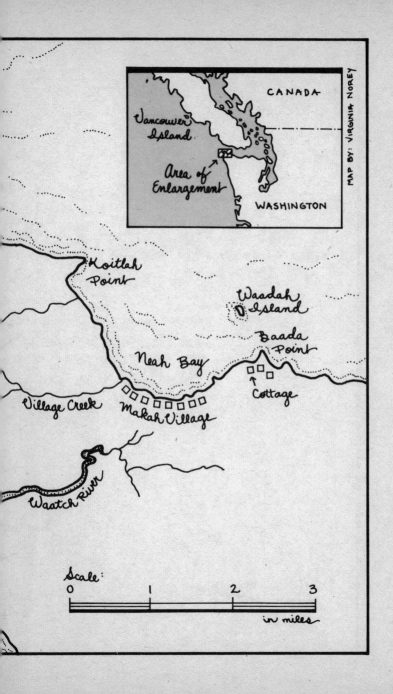

CANADA

Vancouver
Island

Area of
Enlargement

WASHINGTON

MAP BY: VIRGINIA NOREY

Koitlah
Point

Waadah
Island

Baada
Point

Neah Bay

Cottage

Village Creek

Makah Village

Waatch River

Scale:

0   1   2   3

in miles

GHOST CANOE

·1·

Footprints on the Shore

"Nathan, it's time."

He didn't hear. Nathan MacAllister was so deeply asleep, he was like a stone plunging to the bottom of the sea.

"Nathan, it's time."

This time he heard the voice, far away, and then felt the hand on his shoulder. He fought himself back to the surface and awoke. Blinking, he took in his father's face, saw the rain dripping through the tangles of his silver beard. Nathan heard the wind shrieking outside and the rain in sheets lashing the windows, and then he heard his mother coughing in her sleep in the next room. Her cough was getting worse again.

"Your watch, Nathan," came his father's voice, deep

as a foghorn, but gentle. "It's a ghastly night—be careful."

Nathan struggled to his feet and started pulling on his clothes. He thought of the odds stacked against them, and he drew strength from his father's faith in him. "We haven't let the Tatoosh Light fail yet, and we won't," he vowed.

Once he'd wrapped himself in sea-coat, oil slicker, and rubber boots, Nathan pulled his sou'wester over his head and put on his gloves. He took the lantern from his father's hand with the full measure of pride that came from doing the work of an assistant lighthouse keeper at the age of fourteen.

They didn't have any choice. He and his father had to split the night, because they still had the work of four men to do during the day.

"I've lit a fire for the fog trumpet, just in case we need it," his father advised in parting.

Nathan lowered his head and stepped outside into the teeth of the gale. The rain was mixed heavily with salt spray. In a crouch, with one hand clutching the lantern and the other grasping the rail, he fought his way toward the lighthouse. Just before he reached it, against the background of the booming surf he thought he heard the cow downwind, calling as if from a great distance. There was a distinct note of terror in her voice. Then Nathan heard a faint, repetitive sound he identified as the door of her little barn banging.

The cow must be loose in the dark and the storm. Cow, he thought, you better be lying down—there's cliffs whichever way you turn. I can't chase you on a night like this, and neither can my father.

More than once during this winter, he'd been forced by storms to get down on his hands and knees and crawl. Here it was April, and still, wind like this. Would it never end? One of the assistant keepers who'd abandoned them said he'd once been blown clear across Tatoosh Island's treeless, seventeen-acre top before managing to grip onto shrubbery at the edge of the cliff. And that was in the daytime, Nathan thought.

No, I have to tend the light, even if it might mean losing the cow and one of Mother's few comforts, that cup of warm milk three times a day. There might be ships out there depending on this light.

In the foghorn building, he checked the water level in the boiler, then shoveled more coal into the furnace below. No pressure yet on the gauge—no steam. He would check back in half an hour.

Nathan entered the assistants' quarters, which enveloped the base of the lighthouse, and, with his lantern held high, began to climb the spiral stairs. The iron stairway was vibrating uncannily, the way it always did when the wind howled. His hand on the stone wall felt the same vibration. The hair climbed on the back of his neck. He recalled hearing that the roof itself, up above the lantern room, had blown off during a storm several years before.

Near the top of the stairs, he entered the watch room, a small compartment beneath the light. The entire tower was shuddering, and Nathan believed he could feel it swaying. At a time like this back in January, the former assistants had deserted their post here in the watch room, certain that the entire lighthouse was about to collapse into a heap of stone blocks.

When he reached the very top of the stairs, Nathan pulled back the heavy iron door and entered the brilliant lantern room itself. He was amazed, as ever, to be standing so close to the dazzling lens while it was in operation. This was a first-order Fresnel lens, fully twelve feet high, and so wide that when he went inside it during the daytime to clean it, he couldn't touch both sides of the glass, even with his arms spread wide. This miraculous revolving chandelier with its 1,176 prisms was powerful enough to send its sweeping ray twenty miles through the gloom.

Soot was building up on the lens, but no more than usual. Tomorrow they'd get inside and clean every bit of it off. The lamp's five concentric wicks, he could see, were trim and burning cleanly. He checked to see that the clockworks that propelled the light were wound, and he gave the oil machinery another grind to make sure the oil would keep flowing to the wicks. That lighthouse tender ship had better get here soon, Nathan worried, or else there'd be a disaster. The lamp burned ten gallons of oil a night, and they were down to the last fifty gallons.

Everything was in order except for the windows outside the lantern room. They were taking too much salt spray. Even though Tatoosh stood one hundred and fifty feet above the sea, at times like this the waves would batter the ocean-facing side of the island, where the lighthouse was perched, with such fury that the wind swept the spray over the rim of the island, even as high as the top of the tower itself.

Nathan knew it was his job to go outside and clean

4

those windows. The salt spray was griming the glass, and when that happened, the light was so dim it would be hard for anyone at sea to make it out.

It was up to him. His father was asleep, and at this moment he was the operator of the Tatoosh Light at the entrance of the Strait of Juan de Fuca, one of the most treacherous places for ships in all the world, as proven by the wrecks of countless ships on both the American and the Canadian sides.

Nathan wedged the door open—the door latch was broken and he was afraid of it. He went out onto the catwalk and into the howling wind. With one hand he clutched the inside handrail while, with the other, he worked the polishing rag as fast as he could. The wind kept tearing at him and forcing the freezing rain down inside his slicker.

Working as fast as he could, he was halfway around the lantern room when he heard the door slam shut behind him. Almost at the same time, with terrific force, a seabird attracted by the light slammed against the quarter-inch glass only a few feet from his head, and fell dead at his feet. Nathan was startled and unnerved, as he'd been every time this had happened before. It wasn't something he would ever get used to.

He worried about the door, but kept working his way around the lantern. Get the job done, he told himself. He was freezing cold and anxious to get inside as fast as he could. When he got back to the door, he found it had jammed shut, just as he had feared.

Now matter how hard he pulled on the door, Nathan couldn't budge it. Shivering and shaking, he tried to think. Searching for a way down, he considered the lightning-rod cable suspended from the roof above and falling into the darkness below. It would be more than three hours until his father would find him out here. During that time, something might happen to the light, and he wouldn't be able to tend the fog-trumpet boiler, either. Stranded on the catwalk, he might even freeze to death.

Nathan cursed the rusty iron door, and then he cursed the assistant lighthouse keepers. They'd been so sure that the lighthouse tender would steam in soon, bringing their replacements. Little did they know or care that the ship still hadn't come!

He knew what he had to do. Pulling his gloves down tight on his fingers, he reached for the cable, knowing he had to take the risk. *Only thirty feet down to the roof of the house,* he told himself.

Nathan forced himself to lean back away from the tower and try to plant his feet wide against it as he began to lower himself down into the dark. He'd lowered himself down cliff walls this way, and knew he had to keep leaning back, using his feet to work his way down. But the tower was slick and the wind blew him immediately out of position. Then it began to buffet him from side to side, like a pendulum. He felt the cable slipping in his grasp, and his heart jumped wildly in his chest. The salt spray stung his eyes and blinded him.

Don't give up, don't let go!

Suddenly his feet lost their grip on the tower altogether. All his weight was suspended from his hands, and his hands couldn't hold. He was sliding, out of control, down the cable. For a moment he struggled, unsuccessfully, to plant his feet against the tower. Then he managed to wrap his legs around the cable and made a final effort with his hands and feet together to slow himself down.

It worked. He crumpled—rather, crashed—on the peak of the house.

Nathan sprawled on the rooftop, breathing hard. He'd landed on his elbow, and hoped it wasn't broken. He could move it. He wasn't hurt, he'd just scared himself badly.

At last he felt strong enough to work his way along the peak of the house. He reached the ladder that provided access to the roof and the chimneys, and started down. On the ground finally, he collapsed to his knees in relief, then fell back against the building and waited for his heart to slow down.

The wind and the rain were beginning to ebb. Tendrils of fog were creeping off the sea over the rim of the island. No time to dwell on what had just happened—fog could thicken fast.

Nathan climbed the lighthouse stairs, retrieved the lantern, then hurried to the foghorn building. He found the steam level high and ready for service. After stoking the boiler furnace once more, he went to the red engine alongside the huge trumpet-shaped horn that spouted through the wall. Nathan started the engine, opened the drains and exhaust, adjusted the throttle, then slowly opened the valve. The heavy flywheel revolved, and the building shuddered with the deep resounding blast of the horn.

Before his watch was over, fog was pouring up and over the cliffs and beginning to shroud the island. He could take a deeper breath now: all was well with the light and the horn.

In the muffled light of dawn, his father arrived.

Nathan showed him his gloves, torn to tatters at the palms, and told him all that had happened. His father listened carefully, and then Zachary MacAllister said, "You may be just fourteen, but no grown man could've done better."

Together they set out to look for the cow before the fog worsened. Near the north end of the island, they walked to a known danger spot, a strange hole in the ground that always spouted vapor, where countless times Nathan had lain on his belly and watched the sea below thundering through a cave that passed under the island. The hole was just large enough for the cow to have fallen through, but there were no tracks around it this morning.

Nathan and his father scanned the violent surf surging through the offshore rocks as they walked the rim all the way around to the southeast side. The fog was closing the half-mile gap between Tatoosh and Cape Flattery, the storm-wracked northwestern tip of the United States. It was then his father pointed, almost straight down, to the body of the cow on an outcrop of rock at the foot of the cliffs.

Nathan glanced back to his father, who only said, "I suppose all things are difficult before they are easy. Let's go inside and tell your mother."

Fog enclosed the island until it was hidden from view. Nathan and his father spent most of the day cleaning the lens, and they kept the foghorn going. Midafternoon, Nathan's mother called them in for an early supper.

Every so often there was a slight break in the fog and the misty shape of Cape Flattery appeared through the south-facing window. Every twenty-seven seconds came the three-second resounding blast of the foghorn. Nathan had never felt so weary in his life.

As his mother was gazing toward the mainland through one of the brief openings in the fog, her face suddenly registered the utmost astonishment. She pointed toward Cape Flattery. Nathan and his father were shocked by the sight of a three-masted square-rigger under full sail emerging from the mist where a ship never, ever should have been. Like an apparition, the lumber schooner was sailing through the narrow gap between Tatoosh and the mainland.

"They've missed the Strait!" Nathan's mother cried. Nathan and his father went running outside, as fast as they could, toward the edge of the cliff.

They could see the men on the ship, even read the name, the *L. S. Burnaby,* on the side. The sailors were so close Nathan could make out the men's faces, shocked beyond amazement to discover their situation. Paralyzed by the sight of Tatoosh's looming cliffs, the crew stood unmoving on the deck like actors in a tragic drama, staring up at Nathan and his father. A dense bank of fog was engulfing the ship from behind. Only the helmsman was in motion as, realizing their situation, he spun the ship's wheel away from Tatoosh.

Nathan knew instantly what the result of the correction would be. The helmsman was now steering the *Burnaby* directly toward the barely submerged reef known as Jones Rock, invisible in the fog ahead of them.

"Jones Rock!" Nathan exclaimed under his breath. His father had realized the same thing and already

9

was waving the helmsman to steer close under Tatoosh's cliffs, where the schooner would find deep water.

The helmsman saw and understood the waving of the lighthouse keeper's arms. He responded with a frantic reversal of the ship's wheel. Like a scattered flock of sheep, the crewmen were now scrambling this way and that. Moments later, the square-rigger disappeared in the fog, engulfed like a ghost ship.

"What will happen to it?" Nathan asked anxiously, his eyes fixed on the spot where the ship had disappeared.

His father's ruddy features, carved by the sea over decades as he'd stood at the helm of sailing ships, were so grave they reminded Nathan of a minister he'd once seen presiding at a funeral. "God help them," Zachary MacAllister whispered.

Nathan and his parents prayed that night for those sailors, not knowing what had become of them, fearing the worst.

During the night, Nathan and his father again took turns at the watch in the lighthouse. The fog dissolved during Nathan's watch, and the stars came out.

With daylight came no hint that a ship had passed between Tatoosh and the mainland. Filled with relief, Nathan hurried to tell his parents. "They cleared Jones Rock," he said, bursting into the kitchen. "They must have passed safely into the Strait. They're probably in Port Townsend by now."

"It's a miracle," Nathan's mother declared.

His father nodded, then added, "The captain shouldn't have needed a miracle. He should have heard the foghorn."

The next afternoon Nathan and his parents finally learned the sailors' fate from Lighthouse George, the Makah fisherman who delivered their mail once a week in his dugout canoe. The men hadn't been lucky, after all. Lighthouse George said that the ship had foundered in the fog, breaking up on the Chibahdehl Rocks, to the east of Tatoosh, just a few miles past Jones Rock.

The Makahs had found the bodies of fourteen drowned men. And one set of footprints on the shore.

·2·

A Stab Wound to the Heart

Nathan pictured the schooner breaking apart under the feet of the sailors he had seen in their last hour. He could imagine their panic and the shock of the freezing waves. "How could this have happened?" Nathan stammered. "I just don't understand."

"At sea, anything can happen," his father replied.

They helped Lighthouse George as he pulled his fishing canoe a little farther onto the only landing Tatoosh offered, the small beach on its east side.

"Hyas sick tumtum," the Makah said, making a mournful face. "Very sad." Lighthouse George spoke in English mixed with Chinook, the trading jargon that the different Indian tribes used with each other as well as with the Americans and Canadians.

"But didn't they hear the foghorn?" Nathan insisted. "How could they have let themselves get between Tatoosh and Cape Flattery?"

"They'd have heard it," his father agreed. "But they must have become disoriented somehow. Fog can play tricks on you, and so can the currents at the mouth of the Strait. From the sound of it, there was a survivor. We'll soon hear ·how it happened, no doubt—at least as much as that man knows. I pity the captain, but chances are he's beyond pity now."

"Nothing like that ever happened to you, Father," Nathan said. He was immensely proud of his father's long history at sea. At the age of fifty-one, with his commanding height, his thick gray hair and full silver beard, Zachary MacAllister looked every bit Nathan's ideal of a ship's captain. Until his retirement, he had captained the grandest sailing ships ever built, the Yankee clippers. For years he'd worked the trade route from the Atlantic coast of the United States around the horn of South America all the way to China and back.

Captain MacAllister replied humbly, "I had my close calls, believe me. When I made my mistakes, I had luck on my side, and there's no accounting for luck."

Nathan's father prevailed upon Lighthouse George to stay the night on Tatoosh, as George had done several times after delivering the mail when bad weather had prevented his return to Neah Bay. The Makah fisherman hadn't survived into his mid-thirties by taking unnecessary chances, and it would be dark before he'd be able to return home.

Lighthouse George accepted amiably, stooping to

lift a string of three red snappers from the canoe. He brought a present of fish whenever he came, and Nathan's mother especially loved red snapper. After beaching the canoe above the high-tide line, the three walked up the steep path that wound through a break in the cliffs to the grassy top of the island. As he always did, for good luck, Nathan gave a tap in passing to the signpost he'd erected there several months before. With arrows pointing in opposite directions, the sign read in bold letters: WASHINGTON TERRITORY— ½ MILE and CHINA—6,000 MILES. On the back he'd scrawled *Nathan MacAllister, 1874*.

Nathan was pleased to be in the company of Lighthouse George, whose gentle voice and easygoing manner understated the power of the man that was evident in his canoe strokes. On the days the mail was to come, Nathan kept a lookout for him from the rim of Tatoosh, and then ran down the trail to be ready to help with his landing. The fisherman steered deftly through the tricky waters swirling between Tatoosh and Cape Flattery in a graceful canoe fashioned from a single cedar log.

Running ahead of the two men into the house and using his favorite term from his limited Chinook vocabulary, Nathan called to his mother, "A guest for *muck-a-muck!*" The phrase meant just about anything having to do with food that a person wanted it to mean. His mother was delighted to have a guest. "And look what you've brought!" she cried. Her pale complexion brightened as she laid eyes on the red snappers.

"How you do, Beth-Mac," George said to Nathan's mother. A gentle smile spread across his rugged, dark face as he removed his hat made from woven strips of cedar bark. Somewhere George had learned the custom of doffing his hat in the presence of a lady. His black hair spilled past his shoulders. Other than his hat, he dressed in white men's clothes, except that he never wore shoes.

Nathan was fond of Lighthouse George's names for them. His mother's was short for Elizabeth Mac-Allister, his father's was "Cap'n Mac," and his own was "Tenas Mac." *Tenas*, in Chinook, meant "little."

After greeting Nathan's mother, Lighthouse George followed Nathan and his father up the iron stairs of the lighthouse to watch them light the lamp, which they always did half an hour before sunset. The three watched as Vancouver Island, often called the Grave-yard after the many shipwrecks along its shores, began to take on a reddish tinge twelve miles across the Strait. Nathan's father happened to mention to Lighthouse George that he was concerned about running out of oil for the lamp.

"How 'bout whale oil, Cap'n Mac?" Lighthouse George suggested.

Zachary MacAllister's bushy gray eyebrows rose with interest. "Sperm whale oil would be excellent, but no other whale oil will do. Is there some at Neah Bay, George?"

"Only *kwaddis* oil," the fisherman replied, shaking his head. "Gray whale. Too bad."

The next morning, Nathan helped Lighthouse George launch his canoe, watching as he sliced his way through the incoming surf with sure and power-ful strokes. A fairly short man, Lighthouse George nonetheless had considerable height from his waist

15

up. He seemed to have been born for the canoe, in which long legs would have been no advantage. Paddling had made his chest and back thickly muscled, as were his neck, shoulders, and arms. Nathan hoped that one day he would take a ride in Lighthouse George's canoe, possibly even paddle the five miles to Neah Bay with him. But he couldn't see how the opportunity would ever come up.

The next day, still no ship appeared on the horizon, no sign of the overdue government lighthouse tender. Nathan was anxious for the new assistant keepers to arrive. He hoped there would be three of them, to bring the station back to full strength. He hoped they would be good men this time. But right now what the station needed more was lamp fuel, or the Tatoosh Light would go dead. The lighthouse tender would also bring more coal for the fog trumpet, plenty of *muck-a-muck,* and a hundred other essentials his father had requested.

At supper they finished the last of the red snappers. His mother's cough was worse, and she wasn't able to finish her supper. Sometimes her cough scared Nathan, and he knew that it scared his father as well. His father poured her a cup of tea, which usually helped.

"With May coming, and summer," she managed apologetically, "I'll put this behind me. I just haven't had a chance to dry out my lungs, I suppose."

"Summer will be raw on Tatoosh," his father replied soberly. "Windy and cold, you know that, Elizabeth. You won't be able to grow much of a flower garden, or your vegetables either, as you could on the coast of California."

16

Nathan knew his mother and his father must wonder if they ever should have left California, but he'd never heard them say it. He'd never said it either.

"Ah, but there's a wild beauty here," she said instead. "Even if the flowers and vegetables might do poorly."

"Elizabeth . . . ," his father said, with a tone that signaled he was about to make a request, an important one.

His mother looked away, and then brought the teacup back to her lips, waiting for what he would say.

"The doctor's house at the Agency in Neah Bay is still sitting empty. They haven't found another doctor, and from all accounts they won't anytime soon. They tell me it's a snug little cottage with two perfectly operating stoves, one for heating and one for cooking. You wouldn't be alone; you'd have Nathan with you. Please, I want you to reconsider, not only for your sake, but for all three of us."

His mother sat up straight, twisting her finger around a strand of dark hair at the side of her face. Her hazel eyes reflected her habitual determination. "I've never been frail—you know that. I still think I can hold out until they build the new quarters here. We've always been together."

It had been nearly five months that his mother had lived in these damp and smoky rooms, and she'd been sick since the end of the first month. Nathan could still remember her face when they'd first come through this door. She'd been crushed with disappointment upon seeing the moss growing inside on the plaster walls, and the soot from the fireplaces over everything. "Well," she'd managed with her brave cheerfulness, "we have some work to do."

His mother was looking at him now. Nathan knew this was not a time to hide his fears for his mother's health. "But that will be another year, Mother," he said, "maybe longer, before the new quarters will be completed. It might be like waiting for the lighthouse tender, only worse."

His mother had heard the quaver in his voice. With a nod of her head, she acknowledged his concern, then gazed out the window for such a long time that she seemed to have left them.

"I just don't like to give up," she said finally, with a half-smile, as her eyes returned to them and to the present. "We were to be the first family to live here. It's apparent that when the head keeper is a bachelor, as they've all been, they just won't stay. How many head keepers have there been since this light was commissioned in '57?"

"Eleven," his father admitted. "Twelve in seventeen years, counting me. But none of that matters compared to your health."

"I'll pray on it this evening," his mother said. "Nathan, what do you think?"

His reply was simple. "You need to get well, Mother. I've heard it's warmer some in Neah Bay. Drier, too."

His father nodded. "That's what they say."

"We'd be leaving your poor father on Tatoosh, with bachelors who will probably be much more adept at spitting, chewing, and smoking than they are at cooking."

She'd made them laugh, but it was short-lived laughter. Nathan was certain she hadn't been swayed, that she would insist on staying at the lighthouse. He was as afraid of having his family split apart as his mother was. But he was even more afraid for his mother's health. She was only thirty-four years old, much younger than his father. His mother had always been strong. She shouldn't be so sick.

Nathan was surprised the following morning by his mother's decision. Over breakfast, she said calmly, "We can have Lighthouse George bring the vegetables we grow to your father every week, and some flowers, too, when he brings the mail. Your father is right, Nathan. The village will be a better place for us."

As they began their preparations for the move to Neah Bay, the watch continued for the lighthouse tender, which failed to arrive the next day or the next. They were surprised, however, by the sight of Lighthouse George nearing Tatoosh in one of the "great canoes," as Nathan had heard them called. The canoe was more than thirty feet long and paddled by eight men.

To Nathan the great canoe seemed an apparition from ancient times. Its high tapering prow lifted above the waves, carved with the likeness of a wolf's head, as if the entire canoe behind it were a charging, wave-riding sea wolf. Nathan spotted George at the rear of the canoe, seated against the squared-off stern. He was ruddering with his paddle and leading the high-pitched, eerie singing that the others used to time the strokes of their paddles.

Lighthouse George brought news of the lighthouse

tender, the steamship so long delayed. Dockside in Portland for mechanical repairs, it wouldn't sail for yet another week.

Lighthouse George also brought one hundred gallons of pure sperm whale oil for "Cap'n Mac." The Makahs had paddled the great canoe from Neah Bay all the way across the Strait of Juan de Fuca to the Canadian port of Victoria on Vancouver Island, in order to find sperm whale oil. There was undisguised satisfaction in their faces as they watched Nathan's father's astonishment, both at the feat of crossing the Strait in an open canoe and at the gift itself.

The Makahs would accept no payment for the oil. George insisted this was *potlatch,* the Chinook word for gifts and the giving of gifts. Nathan had heard about the legendary gatherings called potlatches in which they were said to give away nearly everything they owned. This gift-giving was their greatest pleasure, his father had told him, and the faces of these Makahs, as they gave the whale oil, showed this to be true.

Before the Makahs left, Nathan asked Lighthouse George if there was any more news about the ship that had wrecked. An hour hadn't gone by without Nathan puzzling over the wreck of the *Burnaby* and the meaning of the footprints. It was going to trouble him until he'd made some sense of it. He wondered if this had been an ordinary shipwreck, or if something strange might have happened, something mysterious.

George seemed reluctant to speak of the *Burnaby,* but at last he did. *"Hyas cultus,* Tenas Mac," he said, as he raked the back of his hand against his chin whiskers. "It's very bad."

"Was the survivor found?"

Lighthouse George shook his head. No survivor had been found, but another body *had* washed up on shore, he told them. But not between Cape Flattery and Neah Bay, where the others were found. This one was discovered about thirty miles south of Cape Flattery, near the Makah village of Ozette. The body was removed by sea to Port Townsend, where it was identified by the owner of the *Burnaby* as that of the captain of his ship.

"But he didn't drown," George said. "He died of a stab wound to the heart."

·3·

A Thief in the Night

Nathan shut the door of their new cottage in Neah Bay quietly behind him. His mother was sleeping, and even though she'd wanted to see him off, he knew it was important to let her rest. In the middle of the night, he'd awakened and found her writing a letter by the light of the kerosene lamp in her room as she muffled the sound of her cough with a handkerchief.

In a few minutes he'd put Baada Point behind him, where their cottage sat on a bluff seaward of the government buildings of the Indian Agency. The sun was rising behind him and it cast his shadow far ahead on the beach. He walked along the sweep of Neah Bay toward the Makah village. His eyes focused on the Makah canoes in the distance, between the beach and the cedar-plank longhouses where Lighthouse George and most of the Makahs lived. Some of the fishermen were already launching their canoes.

Nathan was heading for the trading post to meet up with Lighthouse George, and he was carrying the big Makah basket that George's wife, Rebecca, had given his mother. Its bottom half was filled with clothing for his father on Tatoosh—some his mother had just made and some she'd mended—and the top half was full of baked goods for his father and the new men. Her letters to him, one per day, were tucked in between.

When Nathan arrived at the trading post, he found Lighthouse George already there, sitting at the table in front of the counter. He was having coffee with Captain Bim, the huge owner of the trading post, a bear of a man who was talking excitedly in English spiced with Chinook. Lighthouse George saw Nathan at the door. A happy smile spread across the Makah's face, which brought one to Nathan's as well. Today was the day he'd go out in a canoe with George, and Nathan could barely contain his excitement.

"Come in, come in!" cried Captain Bim, who was the friendliest man Nathan had met in his life, also the biggest talker and just plain the biggest. Even his beard, curly and gray, was enormous. A colony of swallows could nest in it, Nathan mused, perhaps without the trader noticing.

Captain Bim wasn't really a captain at all, Nathan had discovered. He just liked the name, and he liked wearing a nautical cap with an anchor emblazoned on the front. For much of the day, the trader remained seated right where he was, under the sign that read

EVERYTHING FROM NEEDLES TO ANCHORS, where he could readily visit with everyone who came through the door. His Makah assistant, an old man who never seemed to speak, did the legwork around the place and the measuring of tea, coffee, sugar, flour, molasses, and everything else that was kept behind the counter.

Captain Bim's eyes immediately fastened on the baked goods peeking from Nathan's basket. Setting it down beside the table, Nathan brought out three sweet rolls, one for each of them. *"Muck-a-muck,"* Nathan said. Delighted, Captain Bim poured Nathan a cup of coffee, so quickly that Nathan didn't have time to explain that he didn't drink coffee. He decided to follow Lighthouse George's example, and added three spoonfuls of sugar, then waited for the coffee to cool as he savored his sweet roll, bite by flavorful bite.

"I was just telling George that I had a robbery here last night," Captain Bim reported, picking flakes of sugar out of his beard. As he popped the flakes into his mouth and proceeded to lick his fingers, his eyes shifted back to the basket of baked goods, which made Nathan feel a little uneasy.

Nathan took a sip of the coffee. "What did you lose?" Coffee, he decided, wasn't half bad when it was this sweet.

"A Makah fishing harpoon, a whetstone, a good deal of food, some pots and pans, a long length of rope, matches, a hunting knife with an engraving of a clipper ship on the bone handle ... I'm surprised about the harpoon. With all the fish harpoons around Neah Bay, I can't see why someone would have to go and steal one. I just had it up on the wall for looks. You'd

24

think they would've just made their own. If that's the way it's going to be, I might retire to Port Townsend sooner than I expected. I've had in mind to start an ice-cream parlor. . . ."

Captain Bim reached across to the basket and brought out a scone. Nathan wished he hadn't set the basket so close. "Have you had burglaries before?"

"It's been a while—ten, twelve years. That's why I had such a silly little lock on the door. From now on, it will be a great big lock."

With a determined expression, Captain Bim reached for another pastry. Nathan noticed that Lighthouse George had finished his sweet roll, and he remembered about the oil George had brought from Victoria. "Potlatch," Nathan said to George, giving him a scone and taking one for himself.

"A beautiful concept," Captain Bim purred, and took yet another roll with his free hand. They were disappearing as fast as berries into the mouth of a bear.

"I'll be watching everyone who comes into the store," the trader said with his mouth full. "The thief will give himself away; that's what happened last time. The Makahs take care of their own—they humiliated him publicly, and that took care of the problem."

"But what if the thief this time wasn't somebody who lives here?" Nathan suggested on the spur of the moment. He was already considering the possibilities, which was his nature.

"There's nobody here except who's here," Captain Bim proclaimed. "There's nothing but the forest primeval at our backs, Little Mac. No roads in or out. How could there be somebody else?"

"But what about the footprints? The footprints that were found at the time of the shipwreck?"

The trader chuckled and poured Nathan another cup of coffee. "A budding detective! Haven't you heard, young man, that the territorial marshal who came to investigate said those probably were just Makah footprints?"

"What do the Makahs think about that?"

"They say they didn't make the tracks," Bim huffed impatiently, "but who else would be walking barefoot on the beach?"

"Somebody who kicked off his shoes trying to swim to shore!"

Captain Bim laughed as he reached for two more rolls at once. "You have quite an imagination, young man. Don't forget, the ship sank so fast the crew wasn't able to launch any lifeboats. No one *could* have survived, not in those waters. Not a chance. Not a remote chance."

"So who killed the captain?"

"A mutiny, perhaps? The captain could have been a madman. We'll never know. As they say, dead men tell no tales."

Nathan glanced into the basket. Only two rolls left. As a defensive measure, he took the last two. He gave one to Lighthouse George and kept the other for himself.

Lighthouse George caught Nathan's eye and tapped the mailbag lying against his chair. "S'pose we go to Tatoosh?"

"I'm ready!" Nathan declared, standing up quickly. His nerves were buzzing with caffeine.

"Come back soon, Red," the big man declared, standing up as well.

Nathan looked around, confused. "Who's 'Red'?"

"Why, you are."

"I barely have any red in my hair," he protested. "It's mostly brown."

"Aye, but there's red in your cheeks, like your father's. You're a Scot, and Scots are Reds in my book."

Suddenly Nathan felt as though Bim was goading him. Maybe there was something about the jovial trader that wasn't entirely good-natured. It might not be a good thing to let Captain Bim think he lacked a backbone. Keeping his voice as level as he could, Nathan corrected him: "My ancestors were Scots, and I'm proud of it, but I'm an American."

When the huge man replied with a snort, Nathan added, "And please don't call me Red. I just don't like that name."

Bim countered, "I suppose I daren't call you Little Mac, then, since you're too much in your father's tall and sturdy mold to be called little by any means. Will Young Mac do?"

Nathan laughed, and wondered why he'd been so annoyed. Maybe it was the coffee. "Anything but Red!"

He turned to go, but made the mistake of glancing back at the trader. With a friendly slap on Nathan's back, Captain Bim started up again. "It's marvelous having two more English speakers in Neah Bay. You know, I've been here twenty-two years and I don't understand three words of Makah. It's the most difficult language you can imagine. Their own name for themselves is entirely unpronounceable. It's supposed to mean 'People of the Cape and the Seagulls,' which seems rather mundane to me. Makah's a name other people gave to them, and I myself find it far more poetic. . . ."

The trader had talked so fast he'd winded himself, and now he raised his hand to signal them to stay a moment longer.

"Does the word *Makah* mean something?" Nathan asked, to give the trader the chance to draw another breath, and because he wanted to make up for being short with Bim a few moments before.

Captain Bim was pleased that Nathan had postponed leaving for the time being. "It's some nearby tribe's name for them," he continued. "I hear it means 'generous with food,' which they certainly are in my experience. You'd make a good Makah, Young Mac," the trader added with an approving chuckle.

"I'm glad so many people around here speak the trading language, not just Makah. I think I can learn enough of it to talk to people—"

"Ah, that dreadful Chinook," Bim interrupted. "The easiest and most grotesque of languages. All of human expression reduced to a handful of words that mean anything and everything! I try to get George here to use his English when he talks to me—he's one of the few Makah that knows any—but I can't get anything out of him but Chinook. It looks like you've already had better luck!"

Nathan caught a glimpse of George smiling at him. "I'll be back later, Captain Bim," Nathan said cheerfully, scooping up the big basket. But he thought: Not with so much to potlatch next time!

·4·
Fuca's Pillar

As they rounded Koitlah Point, Lighthouse George pointed the canoe west along the rocky, storm-carved shore of Cape Flattery. At the front of the canoe, Nathan paddled with a high heart. Here he was, paddling on the Strait with Lighthouse George in the mailman's dugout canoe! To make everything perfect, it was one of those rare days—the Pacific was living up to its name, the sun was shining, and there was almost no wind.

Lighthouse George guided the canoe outside the line of swells that rose and broke as waves upon the reefs and cliffs along the Cape. Above the shore, white-headed eagles kept watch on the waters from their perches in the tall cedars on the slopes of the mountain. Around the next point, hundreds of gulls were screaming, and Nathan could hear the barking

29

of sea lions. Ahead, like a mighty fortress at the entrance of the Strait, loomed treeless Tatoosh Island. Even on this calm day, its jagged gray cliffs fronted the breaking white attack of the relentless sea. Nathan glanced over his shoulder. George was smiling as he pointed with his face toward the island and said, "Tatoosh."

"I love the sea," Nathan told him.

"The sea is my country, too."

"Where did you learn to speak English?"

"On a whaleship," George replied, with obvious regret in his voice and in his dark eyes. "I was young. I thought, I will go for a year to work on a whaleship. That's what they said—one year—when they took me. Five years later I got back home. They let me off at Vancouver Island—the Nitinat people paddled me home across the Strait."

"Were you ever in the South Seas?"

"Oh yes—all over."

"What job did you have on the ship?"

"Harpoon."

"Harpooner! That's really important! Did you kill a lot of whales?"

Lighthouse George looked away, and when he looked back, his usually amiable face had clouded over with memories that made him look suddenly much older than his years. "Too many, Tenas Mac. Too, too many whales—the seas were red with blood. I was so happy to come back home—never leave again, never, never."

"At least you saw the world," Nathan suggested.

"I saw too much."

The fisherman fell silent as Tatoosh neared. Nathan was hoping this wouldn't be his last day on the water with Lighthouse George.

As they paddled for the tiny beach in the cove on Tatoosh Island's east side, Nathan discovered what a feat it was to bring a canoe through the breaking surf. He paddled, to add speed, but it was George's paddle that knew the language of the waves, not his.

His father, who'd been watching their approach, helped them beach the canoe. Nathan bailed it out with George's small canoe bailer, fashioned from lightweight cedar like everything else the Makahs used, from spoons to great canoes. Nathan had so many things to tell his father, but he began by praising the canoe.

"These canoes are a marvel," Zachary MacAllister agreed. He gave a broad smile. "Their lines are virtually identical with those of the most advanced clipper ships. Look at that long, clean run," he said, with a sweeping wave of his hand. "Look at the hollow entrance, the beautiful shear. I once heard it said that the clipper ships might have been developed from a design that Captain Cook's men brought back from his last voyage. Cook visited these shores almost a hundred years ago when he was searching for the Northwest Passage."

The three ate a meal with the new assistant keepers—two short, one tall, all with mustaches—all looking slightly seasick and hardly more talkative than Lighthouse George, who among strangers was mute as a tree. Nathan was disinclined to talk with the assistant keepers as well. Though he wouldn't have admitted it, he was jealous of their doing the job he had done alone with his father, even if he was happy to be free of it.

Nathan talked softly with his father. He told him how he'd already turned over the soil for his mother's garden, how she was teaching at the Agency every day, showing the Makah girls how to sew on a sewing machine, and how his mother had an order in with Captain Bim for flower and vegetable seed. A steamship called the *Anna Rose* brought supplies once a week from Port Townsend, ninety miles to the east. They should get their seed by the middle of May.

His father was pleased to hear the news. Nathan made him even happier as he went on to tell how his mother and Lighthouse George's wife, Rebecca, had become friends over the sewing machine. Rebecca brought clams she had dug and fish from Lighthouse George, and she wanted to do all the washing for his mother, as well as any other heavy work she could do.

Then Nathan thought of the pastries, and told his father their sad history. His father, who had met Captain Bim previously, enjoyed a hearty laugh, with only mild regret showing in his eyes for the sweet rolls and scones that might have been.

Nathan suddenly remembered the biggest news of all—the burglary of the trading post the evening before—and blurted it all out. "Do you think there might be a connection between the burglary and the murder of the *Burnaby*'s captain?" he concluded breathlessly. "What about the survivor, the man who made the footprints?"

Nathan's father glanced at Lighthouse George, who had been listening but was showing no interest or emotion, and then he stroked his silver beard thought-fully and said to Nathan in measured tones, "It's not impossible that there's a connection, I suppose, but it's highly unlikely. As strange as the wreck of the *Burnaby* was, I can understand that it's troubling you. But let's not leap to conclusions, such as the existence of a survivor. Facts will turn up; they almost always do."

Nathan listened politely, but he couldn't help feel-ing disappointed. His father was so cautious, and Cap-tain Bim lacked all curiosity and had no imagination. It didn't seem right, either, that the marshal who was supposed to investigate had already left. "But Fa-ther," Nathan said. "Fourteen men dead, fifteen counting the captain!"

His father nodded soberly. "Strange circumstances, certainly. Strange goings-on. And the burglary at the trading post . . . I want you to be careful, Nathan, and don't be letting your curiosity get the best of you. Someone may be up to no good in the village, and you must be prudent about where you spend your time."

Lighthouse George, listening intently, interjected, "He's pretty good with that paddle, Cap'n Mac. I could use some help in the canoe. . . ."

Nathan didn't know what to say, but he broke into a smile. He didn't know exactly what George was of-fering him, but he knew the mailman and his wife had become true friends of their family, had adopted all three of them, it seemed. He hoped George meant for him to help with the fishing—his heart beat fast at the thought. He'd work hard, they'd see. He knew he could learn fast.

Before Nathan left with Lighthouse George, he was

able to give his father the rest of the report on his mother. She loved the cottage and working with the Makah girls, and she was as optimistic as ever, but in truth, Nathan reported, her health didn't seem to be improving yet.

"The warmer weather's coming soon," his father said hopefully, and then added, to Lighthouse George, "Thank you for bringing my son as well as the mail. I hope he'll be some help to you."

The brawny fisherman replied with a simple nod of his head.

Nathan helped George launch the canoe into the surf and looked over his shoulder once to catch sight of his father, who was waving good-bye. Then Nathan concentrated, putting all of his strength into his strokes. He wanted to look good for his father. There was a fierce pride burning within him, the pride of being his father's son and feeling at home on the sea.

Instead of heading for Neah Bay, Lighthouse George turned them south through the tricky, tide-driven currents, rough as rapids in a river, that were surging into the Strait and around the tip of Cape Flattery. *"Skookum-chuck,"* George commented, combining the Chinook words for "powerful" and "water." Nathan was amazed to be where he was in such a small craft. *"Skookum,"* Nathan repeated, eyeing the surf breaking against the steep headlands.

They paddled toward the most striking of all the monumental rocks standing offshore. Nathan had often admired it from Tatoosh. It was called Fuca's Pillar—not Two-ca's Pillar as he'd first thought when he'd heard it. A tower of stone, it was named after the Spanish explorer who was given the credit for discovering the strait that now carried his name. The pillar stood like a massive chimney more than a hundred feet above the sea foaming around its base. When he was still on Tatoosh, Nathan had discovered through a spyglass that its flat top was covered with a thick carpet of grass.

Once past Fuca's Pillar, Lighthouse George guided them closer to the cliffs, to a spot where the sea was washing over a reef. Between the canoe and the reef, sea otters were floating on their backs and grooming their fur. One was using a stone to break open a sea urchin. South of the reef, as they paddled the surf line opposite a small sand beach, Nathan saw something barely sticking out of the sand. When they got a little closer, he realized what it was. "A ship's wheel!" he cried, pointing it out to George.

They paddled to shore, and Lighthouse George watched as Nathan dug the wheel out of the sand. None of the steering handles were broken off. The name of the ship—*The Queen of Malabar*—was barely legible in the corroded metal plate at the center of the wheel. "It's old," Nathan said. "I'll bet it's been buried in the sand a long time."

"Let's put it in the canoe," George said. "Cap'n Bim will pay you for old stuff like that."

As they paddled north back toward Cape Flattery, they noticed that a light schooner had anchored offshore and that a rowboat was bobbing in the swells at the base of Fuca's Pillar. A sailor was working the oars, skillfully keeping the rowboat off the rocks, while a man in gentleman's clothing was climbing around on the lowest reaches of the pillar. "What would anyone be doing out there?" Nathan asked as he squinted to get a better look. "It looks like he's searching for something."

"*Mesachie mitlite,*" Lighthouse George said disapprovingly. "That's a place to stay away from. No one goes there."

"Why is it a place to stay away from?" Nathan wondered, watching the man's poor attempts at climbing.

"Something happened there, a long time ago. Before the Boston men and the King George men came in boats big as houses, before that, the Makahs had a contest there. Every year."

Lighthouse George pointed indirectly toward the pillar with a motion of his thumb. "Young men would climb up there."

Nathan took a dubious glance up and down the walls of the pinnacle. He wondered if it might be possible for a climber to wedge himself into the vertical cracks. "Is that possible, to climb the pillar?"

The fisherman shrugged. "Maybe. Boys still climb in cliffs to find eggs."

"I used to do that myself, near the lighthouse where we lived before, but I always started from the top, and I had a rope. I'd bring the eggs for my mother. What kind of a contest was it that they used to have on Fuca's Pillar?"

"The boy who climbs highest, he plants a sign of his clan. Then his clan has good luck for the next year."

"So why is it a bad place?"

"Once, a boy climbed so high, he couldn't go back down. He knew if he tried to go down, he would fall. So he just climbed all the way to the top."

Nathan was staring up at the top of the pillar. He was picturing the Makah boy stranded on its grassy top. He could imagine the boy's fear as he stared straight down, a hundred feet, to the rocks below. It wouldn't have been possible to dive clear of the rocks. "What happened to him?"

"People tried to get him. They even tied rope to birds, hoping a bird would fly over and drop the rope. No luck."

"Couldn't they save him?"

Lighthouse George replied with a mournful shrug. "The boy died up there. That's why it's a place to stay away from."

·5·

A Plume of Smoke

"Do you think that man found what he was looking for?" Nathan wondered, as the man who'd been on Fuca's Pillar got back in the rowboat and was rowed to the schooner.

"Don't know, Tenas Mac," Lighthouse George said with a shrug. As the schooner disappeared around Tatoosh and back into the Strait of Juan de Fuca, Lighthouse George concentrated on paddling through the *skookum-chuck*, the rough water streaming and eddying through the gap between Tatoosh and Cape Flattery. It took constant attention to avoid being swept onto Jones Rock, which was visible in rare moments of calm between the waves.

At the tip of the Cape, monumental seastacks of dark stone battered by the sea stood out in the surf and blocked Nathan's view of the mighty cleft that the sea had carved into the mainland. He knew the cleft was there, and he knew its name—the Hole in the Wall. He remembered it from the maps posted in his father's office out at the lighthouse. As Nathan paddled along, he thought for a moment that he was seeing a thin plume of smoke rising from behind the seastacks, in the vicinity of the Hole in the Wall.

He stopped paddling and tried to get a better look. The next moment, the smoke wasn't there, and he wondered if he'd been mistaken. Nonetheless, he told George that he'd seen smoke behind the rocks. George only shrugged.

"But what if somebody's there?" Nathan insisted. "Maybe somebody really did survive that shipwreck."

Lighthouse George shrugged a second time. "What happened to that ship, that's not our business. Fishing, that's Makah business."

George was paddling with powerful strokes now, and Nathan gave his attention back to his own paddle.

"Let's get some fish," the voice behind him said. "Lotsa fish."

Ahead, Nathan realized, the waters were riddled with splashes, and Nathan could see silver flashing where small fish—herring certainly—were jumping from the water. Then he saw the reason why, as a gleaming black-and-white whale broke the surface. Lighthouse George stopped paddling and they both watched as three, four, five whales breached, sleek and muscular as dolphins. Nathan had seen the playful killer whales only from a distance before, and he'd underestimated their size. They still couldn't compare to the gray whales, but they were longer nose to tail than Lighthouse George's fishing canoe. Such speed and power!

The whales were soon gone, but the herring remained. Lighthouse George had Nathan, keeping low, switch places with him. At the rear of the canoe now, Nathan paddled George toward the water seething with herring. The fisherman took a pole from the bottom of the canoe. Its last several feet were studded with bones as long as a man's little finger and as sharp as needles.

As soon as the canoe was among the herring, Lighthouse George began raking the water with the pole, almost as if he were paddling with it. With the first stroke he impaled seven or eight herring, and now he knocked the pole on the edge of the canoe, dropping the herring inside. In an hour of work, with Nathan paddling and the powerful Makah raking the water, they had half filled the canoe with fish. "Lotsa fish!" Nathan declared.

Rebecca was there among the women along the shore handling the herring from earlier canoes. Nathan ran to Captain Bim, who was watching the spectacle of the village taking in the herring run.

"Captain Bim," he reported breathlessly, "I saw some smoke behind the rocks out at the tip of Cape Flattery!"

"Yes . . . ?" Captain Bim replied.

"Couldn't the smoke be from the burglar's campfire? Remember, the robber took matches!"

The trader had his eye on the old ship's wheel that still lay across the gunwales of Lighthouse George's canoe. "You've found an interesting piece of flotsam there. Did you find a name on it?"

"*Queen of Malabar.*"

Captain Bim scratched his beard appreciatively. "She wrecked on the Graveyard, over on the Vancouver Island side of the Strait, back in '53."

"Will you pay me for it?"

"Yes, I will, but maybe not as much as you're thinking."

"What about the smoke I saw?"

"Did George see it?"

"Only me—it didn't last long."

Captain Bim was walking down to take a closer look at the old wheel.

"But what if there is someone there, and he's the burglar?" Nathan insisted.

"Then he'll have his head blown off next time he breaks in. I'm sleeping in the store."

The trader hemmed and hawed over the ship's wheel and finally agreed he'd pay two dollars. Nathan knew it wasn't a bad price. "What else will you pay for—what kind of stuff should I be looking for?"

"Well, I pay two bits for the bricks from the old Spanish fort that stood east of where the Agency is now. Those bricks are a rarity. You see, they're all that's left of the fort. Those are artifacts of true historical significance, the kind of thing I can sell."

"The Spanish actually had a fort here?"

"Indeed they did, Young Mac. Late 1700s. They were contending with the English at the time for control of the Northwest, before the Americans got into the act. Lots of bad blood between the Spanish and the Makahs."

"Did they fight?"

"They say the Spanish had six cannons at the fort, several of them trained on the village."

"I thought the Makahs were peaceful."

Captain Bim gave a great snort, like a trumpeting elephant, and his jowls shook. "These people wouldn't still be here today if they hadn't descended from warriors. The Makahs in the old days had to be able to hold their own against fleets of sixty-foot war canoes that could swoop down on them at any moment. Some of those tribes way up to the north were nothing less than fierce."

"So what happened with the Makahs and the Spanish?"

"The Spanish had those big guns, as I said. But it was the English who finally ran the Spanish off, or at least that's what you'll read in the history books. The Makahs claim they did it themselves and burned the fort. All that's left these days are a few flat yellow bricks from the fort's bakery—about eight inches long, five inches wide, and an inch thick."

Nathan was picturing finding lots of bricks. "Two bits a brick?"

"You'd be lucky to find any. Best chance might be if that creek over there changes its course and digs 'em up for you."

"I'll keep my eyes open."

"Well, while you're looking around..." The big man lowered his voice, though there was no one very close. "There's an account—no more than a legend, I suppose—that the Spanish commander, fearing capture at sea, buried a fortune in gold bullion some-

42

where around Cape Flattery before he and his men abandoned the fort."

"Do you believe this story yourself?"

"Implicitly!" the trader thundered. "The gold wouldn't have originated here, you see; it would have been transported from the Spanish empires far to the south. The Spanish commanders all over the New World melted down the golden art of the Indies into bars, and then, of course, everywhere they went they had to carry their plunder with them. No safekeeping until they could get it back to Spain."

Captain Bim's eloquence had winded him. He paused for several gulps of air, then remembered something. "The captain's brother was here today," he continued. "Jeremiah Flagg was his name. On a boat chartered out of Port Townsend. He's already gone."

"Your brother?" Nathan wondered, completely confused.

"No, no, the brother of Alexander Flagg, the murdered captain of the *Burnaby*. And his visit surely got off to a bad start. To begin with, neither the captain's brother nor the crew of his chartered ship would accept the help of the Makahs. The Makahs had paddled out to bring them ashore by canoe, as is the custom at Neah Bay, with the surf as tricky as it is. The gentleman wouldn't pay the customary fee, which is modest, and then he paid the price—oh, did he ever pay the price, he and the sailor bringing him ashore. Their rowboat was caught by a wave.... I saw it turn end over end."

The trader couldn't resist a smirk and a gleeful chuckle. "A perfect loop-the-loop!"

"What happened then?"

"The Makahs plucked them from the sea, of course, which they always do free of charge. Once ashore, our visitor, in addition to being out of temper, was quite mysterious. Wanted to know about every bit of flotsam and jetsam the Makahs had recovered from the wreck. The Makahs believe in 'finders keepers' when it comes to gifts of the sea that wash up on their beaches. After all, that's the law of Washington Territory as well as their custom. And besides, picking up salvage from white men's ships that come to grief on their shores is one of the Makahs' great pleasures in life."

"I wonder what the captain's brother was looking for?"

"He wouldn't say. I'm not sure he knew exactly. Abrupt and abrasive he was—not a sympathetic person in the least, and utterly unschooled in the art of conversation. He stuck his nose into cedar boxes full of oil and boxes of dried fish. He was after some small object, would be my guess. I showed him everything I had in the store that came from the wreck, in case he cared to buy it—for the right price, you understand.

"Before he left, he wanted me to tell him 'where Makahs would never go.' A mysterious question, mysteriously asked. For a price, being a trading man, I told him that place would be Fuca's Pillar, because of a long-held superstition."

Captain Bim took a twenty-dollar gold piece from his pocket and held it up for Nathan's inspection. "Not a bad return for such a common bit of knowledge."

"But what if that Spanish gold you just told me about is hidden there? What if he finds it?"

"Oh, no chance of that. I've scoured the place myself. Nothing there."

Nathan guessed Bim hadn't looked very high on the pillar.

"Well, back to work and late for dinner," Bim concluded.

"What about your robbery? Do you have any suspects yet?"

"One, I suppose," Bim replied with a chuckle. "Or a race of them."

"What? Who?"

"At dusk last night, a pack of small children came screaming in from the woods. They claimed to have seen the 'One Who Lives in the Woods.' "

"What's that?"

"A wild man they believe in. Sometimes they call him the 'Hairy Man.' I gather he's a cannibal. Sometimes I get the idea there's supposed to be a whole race of them."

Captain Bim didn't seem to be in jest. "Have you seen this 'Hairy Man,' Captain Bim?" Nathan asked. "You've been here more than twenty years."

"Glimpses," the trader replied in all seriousness. "I suppose it's just a tale the Makah use to keep their children out of the woods, especially at night, but let me tell you this, young man ... only a fool goes off exploring in this godforsaken wilderness. You and I have no idea what's out there."

·6·

An Eternal View of the Sea

In the morning it was gray and grim outside. Lighthouse George hadn't come for him, as Nathan had hoped he would. It had drizzled off and on during the night, and now, for the time being at least, it had quit. Standing by the window, looking out to sea, Nathan realized he'd been paddling around Cape Flattery with Lighthouse George all night in his dreams. All night he'd been paddling hard to get by Jones Rock and glimpsing that plume of smoke behind the rocks. All night he'd been puzzling over the smoke. Captain Bim and the territorial marshal from Port Townsend were convinced that no one on board the *Burnaby* could have survived the wreck. But what if they were wrong?

Nathan stared at a canoe out in the bay. The graceful canoe was disappearing into the mist in the direction of Waadah Island, only a mile offshore but invisible this morning. Could that be Lighthouse George? Nathan wondered. Would he go out fishing on a day like this? Without knowing the answer, Nathan felt left behind. Nothing in the world compared to navigating the waters of the Strait in George's canoe!

"You're restless," his mother said from her rocking chair. She was reading *The Tempest,* by William Shakespeare.

"That's for sure," he agreed.

"You could read a good book. What about *Robinson Crusoe?* It's a perfect day just to stay warm and tend the fire, don't you think?"

"It's not really raining," Nathan said. "The drips off the roof are from the fog."

"I know. There's just so much moisture in the air."

"I'm glad you're staying indoors today. How do you feel?"

"Warm," she said. "Comfortable. Content."

Nathan was pleased that his mother felt warm. On Tatoosh, that had never really been possible. For him, the cottage felt too snug this morning. With the coal heater radiating so much warmth and the embers glowing in the cookstove's firebox, it was a wonder his mother could tolerate the blanket over her lap and the shawl around her shoulders.

"I feel more like exploring," he told her. "It's spring-time, even if it doesn't feel like it. Captain Bim will pay two bits for every brick I can find from an old Spanish fort. Besides, I'd like to take a look around."

His mother understood how hard it was for him to stay inside. "Dress warmly," she said. "And pack a lunch in case you stay out. We have bread and cheese, and dried cod from Rebecca. Take a few boiled eggs and an orange."

"I'll put some tea water on for you." Nathan leaned down and kissed his mother on her forehead. Her skin was fragile, like her delicate pastry crusts. "Thanks," she whispered. He took the empty coal scuttle outside and filled it from the bin, then replaced it by the stove for her.

He dressed quickly for the raw day. In just a few minutes his lunch was packed and he was bundled in the same foul-weather gear, down to his rubber boots, that he wore on Tatoosh. He slung his satchel over his shoulder and fitted his waterproof sou'wester over his head.

"Hope you find a ton of bricks," his mother said.

"Or Spanish gold!" he declared. "I probably won't be back until dark, unless the weather turns awful."

Nathan walked east at first, along the shore and away from the Agency buildings. Past Baada Point, he found the creek Captain Bim had told him about. According to Captain Bim's story, the fort had stood on the headlands near the creek's mouth, yet he couldn't find the slightest trace of it. He began to suspect that it was purely legendary. Nonetheless, he kept his eye peeled for the yellow bricks that were supposed to be vestiges of the fort's bakery. He paid extra attention as he waded up the creek bed, starting from its mouth on the beach. Here and there he leaped the creek when he needed to cross. Perhaps no one had looked for bricks since the last big rains.

At last he found one in the creek bed, exactly the sort of brick Captain Bim had described. Flat, thin,

GHOST CANOE

yellowish, about eight inches long. So the Spanish had been here after all!

He was certain he'd find more bricks. But after a half hour's search up and down the creek, he hadn't added any to his satchel. He realized he hadn't even been thinking about the bricks. All the while he'd been thinking about that plume of smoke out near the tip of Cape Flattery. The smoke had come from the base of the cliffs, behind the rocks. It should be possible to walk all the way out to the tip of the Cape and investigate. From above the cliffs, it might be possible to see smoke and to look down and see where it was coming from.

Maybe he'd find a column of water vapor that only looked like smoke, formed perhaps by the peculiar action of the surf constricted in a crevice. But *something* had made that plume. And he had to know.

To avoid being detained by the talkative Captain Bim, Nathan steered wide around the trading post and kept to the back of the longhouses. The poles of the drying racks all stood empty, the fish having been taken inside to be strung high above the cookfires. A few ravens were walking around, picking up the scraps. Only a couple of naked little kids and a few old women in their long dresses and shredded cedar-bark capes saw him pass, but they ignored him. With the exception of Lighthouse George, the Makahs never seemed to wave, even to each other.

Even the young Makahs his own age looked past him. Once in a while he got a shy smile. If he really learned to speak Chinook, it might be different, he thought. It was a lucky thing George could speak English. He was thankful for Lighthouse George. Neah

49

Bay would feel so strange and lonely if he didn't have him. His mother must feel the same way about Rebecca.

With swampy ground sucking at his boots, Nathan picked up his step and soon entered the dark, dripping forest of giant spruce, fir, and cedar. From somewhere nearby came a dull, repetitive pounding. After winding around the hill toward the sound for several minutes, Nathan came upon a team of Makahs working on one of the massive cedars. Two men and two boys were standing around the base of the ancient tree looking up at two men working above, who were perched on logs that had been leaned up against the big cedar.

Nathan recognized the two men on the ground. The white-haired old man with abalone-shell earrings had been among those in the canoe when Lighthouse George brought the whale oil for the lighthouse. Another man, with a wispy gray beard, was known as Young Carver, even though he wasn't young.

Almost every day Nathan had paused by the village creek just up from the beach, where Young Carver was making one of the great canoes. The canoe-maker was a man of great seriousness and dignity. Nathan had tried at first to speak to him, greeting him with a few words of Chinook, but Young Carver had made it apparent he didn't want to talk. That's the way it had been with all the Makah except Lighthouse George and Rebecca. No one was unfriendly; it was more like he was invisible, even to the children.

The men and the boys working on the tree acknowledged him now, with the faintest signals. One nodded; one might have smiled. They continued to talk among

themselves in their own language. He didn't understand even a syllable of Makah. He tried to fathom
what the two above were doing, as they pounded on
long wooden wedges with hand-held stone mauls.

Previously, Nathan could see, two horizontal
notches had been chopped a quarter of the way into
the tree. One of the deep notches was five or so feet
above the ground, the other a full twenty feet higher
and directly above it. The men up in the air were
stripping a plank from the living tree between the two
notches. This, he realized, was how the planks on the
longhouse walls and roofs had been made. These
Makahs were making lumber!

Fascinated, Nathan sat on a log and watched. The
men and boys on the ground, in pairs, began to pull
on ropes that had been looped over the high end of
the plank, already freed from the trunk with the
wedges. Bit by bit they were prying the plank of green
wood away from the tree.

When the four at last freed a plank, and it came
falling to the ground, Nathan applauded. They looked
at him strangely, as if they had never heard applause
before. Nathan felt foolish.

"Tenas Mac," Young Carver said with a friendly
smile, surprising Nathan.

Grateful that the dignified canoe-maker had acknowledged him, Nathan opened up his satchel and
asked, *"Muck-a-muck?"* He proceeded to spread the
contents on the log: a loaf of bread, three boiled eggs,
a hunk of cheese, the dried cod, the orange. "Generous with food," he remembered. He gestured with his
hand for them to join him.

He sat in a circle with the Makahs, and they ate,

speaking softly in their own language. None of them reached for the orange. That would be his lunch, he realized. The Makahs weren't dressed nearly as warmly as he, but they didn't seem to be cold either. They didn't attempt to speak any more Chinook with him, so he didn't try it with them. When they had finished the food, they didn't thank him. But as he walked away, he saw several bob their heads, and the old man with the white hair repeated his name: "Tenas Mac."

Nathan retraced his footsteps to where he had first entered the forest and began to climb. Captain Bim had warned him to stay out of the woods, but he had always prized being off on his own outdoors. As he plunged deeper into the forest, he noticed, here and there, the profiles of living cedars with vertical portions of their trunks missing. Most of the scars on the ancient trees were themselves ancient, healed over and covered with moss. The Makahs, Nathan realized, went to their trees for lumber as if they were milking cows. The trees kept on living. The Makahs could always come back for more.

For an hour or more he climbed up the steep mountainside, here and there crossing faint trails. He climbed so high that he entered the cloud that for much of the winter, from Tatoosh, he'd seen clinging to the summits of the twin mountains above Cape Flattery.

It was eerily quiet as he walked on the spongy forest floor among the misty, ghostly shapes of the giant trees. He couldn't see to their tops or even a hundred feet ahead of him. But as he reached the summit of the first mountain, he could hear the fog trumpet on

Tatoosh sounding its deep-throated warning, and he realized he could navigate by it all the way down to the tip of the Cape. He also remembered his father's warning about being careful, and he felt a twinge of guilt.

Nathan walked the saddle between the mountains until he stood atop the second summit. He saw nothing, being inside the cloud, but knew exactly where he was. Tatoosh lay directly ahead toward the foghorn. A few degrees to the left, Fuca's Pillar. A few degrees to the right, the Strait of Juan de Fuca. He would bear only slightly to the right of the horn, and that would lead him to the cliffs, above the spot where he'd seen the smoke in the jumble of seastacks.

He wove his way through thickets of salal bushes and salmonberry vines, and alongside a giant, decomposing log that had a row of young cedars growing in an arrow-straight line along its entire length. He happened to glance up through a break in the trees. A familiar yet entirely unexpected shape up in the foggy branches made him stop and stare and wonder if his eyes were deceiving him. Yes, it was really there, twenty feet up in the air, resting on a platform that had been constructed across the branches of a giant spruce: a Makah canoe.

He stood there staring and staring, confounded by the uncanny sight. A hundred other times, he realized, he could've walked right by and never realized it was there.

What the canoe was doing up there, he couldn't begin to imagine. He only knew he had to find a way to get up in the tree and take a closer look.

A hundred yards away he found a young hemlock

that had died for lack of light, then had been uprooted by the wind. He got lost trying to find the canoe again. In this forest, it could be seen only from that certain angle. At last he stumbled across the place again, and succeeded in dragging the young hemlock back to the big spruce. The canoe was still up there, like an apparition in the cloud. He rested, and then he stood the hemlock up, dragged it into position, and lowered it until it rested against the lowest branch of the spruce. It needed a bit of a twist until its own branches locked against the branches of the spruce and kept it stable.

Nathan threw off his oil slicker and even his sou'wester. He was a strong climber, but he needed to climb unencumbered. Up the hemlock he went, hand over hand, until he stood on the lowest branch of the spruce. He caught his breath, and then he climbed up to the level of the canoe.

His first glimpse inside caught him completely unprepared, and took his breath away. He was looking at an ancient human skeleton, including the skull, in the rear of the canoe. The bones had crumpled into something of a heap, but Nathan could still make out the shape, the arms, the legs, the ribs, as they might have looked if they'd still been connected to each other. The handle of a canoe paddle rested close by the bones of a hand. The paddle was covered with moss and badly decayed. The canoe itself was spongy and entirely covered with a thick blanket of moss.

His eyes went back to the empty eye sockets of the skeleton. Like everything else in the forest, they and the entire skeleton had a greenish cast. He had seen the bones of animals before, but never the skeleton of

a human being. This is bad, he thought. *Hyas cultus*—
I shouldn't be here! Though every nerve in his body
was buzzing, he told himself not to be afraid.

Curiosity made him linger. A coil of rope caught his
eye, heavy rope like he'd seen back in the village. He
couldn't tell what it was made from—perhaps cedar
bark and some sort of animal sinew braided together.
The rope was badly decayed. Alongside the coil of
rope lay a hefty spear more than a dozen feet long.
The spearhead was fashioned of mussel shell, with
twin antler tips, like barbs, attached at the base. Next
to the spear lay a wooden club carved in the image of
a seal. Near the club a large round hole had apparently been punched in the bottom of the canoe. Drops
of water were falling through it to the forest floor
below.

Nathan wanted to reach for the spear and the club
and take them in his hands. They looked firm enough
to handle without breaking. But he would have had
to leave the tree branch where he was standing, and
get out on the planks that supported the canoe. They
appeared to be too rotten to hold him.

He was about to turn and go when the unnaturally
square shape of a small box caught his eye, just behind the skeleton at the very rear of the canoe, very
close to where he was standing. Carefully, he reached
down for the box. His fingers could barely reach that
far, but he was able to grasp it and retract it without
touching the bones.

The box, unlike the canoe, was still sound. Shielded
from the rain by the wide seat used by the paddler at
the stern of the canoe, the small cedar box had been
preserved over untold decades. For a moment he

thought he shouldn't look in the box—there might be something gruesome inside.

I'll just take a peek, he told himself. As he held the box to his belly, his fingers pried at the lid.

Finally it came loose. He was relieved to see two innocent-looking objects fashioned from bone: smooth cylinders, about two and one-half inches long, shaped like miniature barrels. Toward the ends, each was ringed with two rows of tiny circles that had dots in their centers. One of the cylinders was banded around its middle with countless wraps of fine black string of some kind; the other was all bone. He took the unwrapped one in his fingers and felt its smoothness. It was yellow with age and shiny, perhaps from long handling. It felt like it was made to be handled.

The bone cylinders had been kept perfectly dry through the years by the integrity of the cedar box. They were in perfect condition. Lighthouse George would know what they were. If he were to take one, just to learn what it was, he could always put it back.

I can describe it without taking it, he told himself. What would George think if I took something from a Makah grave?

The answer was obvious. He replaced the small cedar box with its two bone cylinders exactly where he'd found it, careful once again not to touch the skeleton.

Nathan took one last look at the canoe. Its high, curving prow was carved in the image of a man-bird, with tall ears that stood atop its head. As the foghorn on Tatoosh gave another of its deep three-second blasts, he realized that the canoe was pointed directly at the open ocean. The man had been buried so he would be looking eternally out to sea.

·7·

A Glimmer in the Dark

Every twenty-seven seconds came the blast of the fog-horn on Tatoosh. Bearing slightly to the right, Nathan steered toward it as he descended to the tip of the Cape. Behind him, the forest had swallowed up the burial canoe, and he had to convince himself that he had not dreamed it.

He had misgivings—about looking for the plume of smoke, about what he might find, about being so far from the village. He had misgivings now about this strange forest itself. It was brooding and dark and mysterious, and if it wasn't evil in itself, it was a perfect place for evil to hide. A shiver ran through his bones as he paused and looked all around. He thought about returning to the cottage as quickly as possible.

Be brave, he told himself. And be alert. There's no

evil in the forest. Evil, as his father had pronounced many times before, lurks only in the hearts of men.

Before he could see the seastacks offshore, he could hear the surf pounding them. Be careful you don't walk right off the cliffs, he told himself.

It didn't really make sense that a man could be living out at the tip of Cape Flattery. It had been several weeks since the wreck of the *Burnaby*. Why wouldn't a survivor have made his way to the village?

Because he killed Captain Flagg, came the inescapable answer. He's biding his time until he can get away. It's not so easy to escape when no roads lead into the interior, a vast and impenetrable wilderness.

No one else will believe it, Nathan told himself, unless I find something, see something.

The trees began to decline in size and number as he got closer to the sea. As he reached the bluffs above the cliffs, he found them stunted and windblown, leaning drastically inland. Now he could begin to see the jumble of colossal seastacks offshore that were remnants of the former mainland. Some of the giant rocks were crowned with living trees. Keeping the Strait on his right and fighting his way through devil's club and salal bushes, he came to a place where the view opened as the cliff bent sharply inland.

Nathan found himself standing above a cove behind the seastacks, where the sea had carved a spearpoint-shaped defile hundreds of yards into Cape Flattery's headlands. This hidden cove, he realized, was the Hole in the Wall. He was looking hundreds of feet right down into it. It was a wild and tumultous scene below, as the foaming sea, thick with waving, uprooted bull kelp, rushed through massive cave-tunnels in the seastacks and surged against the base of the cliffs.

Nowhere did he see a beach or any place that would shelter a human being. The plume of smoke, he admitted now, had been purely a figment of his imagination. But he couldn't see all of the hidden cove from where he was standing, so he decided to go on a little farther to see if it might be possible to gain a different vantage point.

Where the cliffs turned back in the direction of the sea, he found a creek plunging through a break in the cliffs. If he could follow the path of the creek, he realized, it would take him all the way down to salt water.

Before long, the creek tumbled over a rock face and plunged down a waterfall. He was stopped, unless . . . To his right, something had caught his eye, something vaguely unnatural. A bit closer and he realized he was looking at ancient, moss-covered stone stairs leading down into the Hole in the Wall.

The skin on the back of his neck felt suddenly like it was being pricked with needles. He looked all around, full of apprehension. Quit making yourself afraid, he thought, and started down the stairs, quietly, cautiously.

The stairs brought Nathan around and below the waterfall. Now he could see the surf lapping, far below, against a tiny beach of dark sand. He proceeded down the ravine alongside the roaring creek, arresting his descent by clinging to roots and downed trees that had been toppled by the wind. Nowhere did he see a skid mark on the soggy slope, or even a place where the moss had been disturbed. He was reassured that he wasn't about to surprise a murderer. But still, he wanted to make it all the way down to sea level, to see what it would be like down in the hidden cove behind the rocks and below the secret stairs.

At last he stood on the beach. It was no more than a hundred feet long, only a narrow strip with the tide high, as it was now, and it didn't have a footprint on it, or a shelter of any kind, or even the smell of smoke. At last he breathed easy, and he walked along the waterline, picking his way through driftwood and kelp. His eyes were drawn to the surf pounding its way toward shore through the caves in the monumental seastacks. He could see three caves right from where he was standing.

Nathan's eyes returned to the beach at his feet, and he realized he was looking at bits of charcoal, barely above the waterline, left behind by the ebbing high tide. They hadn't been noticeable at first against the dark sand, but they were there.

Did the charcoal wash here all the way from Neah Bay? Or did it wash down a creek and into the sea?

He walked to the west end of the beach, where a rocky outcrop extending from the cliff prevented him from proceeding any farther. Or did it? He was a good climber.

He'd leave his oil slicker behind; it was much too cumbersome. If he could just get up on that outcrop and take a look beyond . . .

Nathan wasted no time. The day was getting on now, and he'd have to start back soon and hurry all the way to make it home before dark. He scrambled up and up until he was looking around the corner at another small beach. This one had a cave in the cliff at the far end. He looked for footprints along the shore, but the beach looked pristine, as if it had never been walked upon.

He almost turned back, but then he realized there was a way to get down to the second beach. It wouldn't take but a few minutes to go look at that cave. Once down, he walked the beach, finding more charcoal along the sand and in the waves lapping the shore. At the entrance of the cave, he found himself looking at a pile of clam and mussel shells just inside. He wondered what creature would bring clams and mussels here, to break them open in the shelter of a cave. A raccoon, he decided, or possibly a bear. It had to be something clever with its hands.

The cave, he suddenly realized, smelled of wood-smoke. But his mind was working too slowly to stop his feet. Another step into the darkness and he felt his rubber boot crunch something underfoot. He knelt and turned the other direction, toward the light, to see what it was. Charcoal. Suddenly his heart was pounding in his ears.

Nathan spun around, peering into the darkness again. He heard, or believed he heard, the sound of breathing, someone or something breathing. Straining to hear, he stopped breathing himself.

Now he heard nothing at all.

A full minute later he heard the breathing sound begin again, faint yet unmistakable. Whoever, whatever it was, was close, much too close.

Then he saw, as his eyes were becoming accustomed to the near darkness, a glint of metal. It was hard to tell, but he thought it might be a knife he was seeing. The knife was slowly being raised by a shadowy arm attached to the barest-perceptible silhouette of a man with a shaggy beard and a huge head of hair.

There . . . the glimmer of two eyes in the dark!

He fought the impulse to turn and run. His best chance was to pretend that he had heard nothing, seen nothing. He shrugged and, with his heart hammering, slowly turned his back on his danger, and walked out of the cave and into the light.

Only once, when Nathan was climbing the rock outcrop at the end of the beach, did he look back. He was sure he would see a man with a knife at the cave entrance. He saw nothing.

Still, when he dropped from the outcrop to the first beach and collected his oil slicker and sou'wester, he broke into a run. All the way up the steep ravine, he climbed as fast and as hard as he could. He never looked back. When at last he reached the ancient stairs that led around the waterfall and up to the top of the cliffs, he finally stopped to gulp air. He looked back down the way he had come, expecting the man to be pursuing him. Nothing.

Once atop the cliffs, Nathan took off at a dead run, keeping the sound of the sea on his left. He never stopped running. In his haste he couldn't find trails to follow, even game trails. It was getting murky under the canopy of the ancient trees. Dark was coming on fast. He clawed his hands through thickets of devil's club, salal, and salmonberries. At last he could hear a dog barking in the distance. He was getting close to Neah Bay and his mother's cottage. He kept running. It was an utter shock when, in the near dark under the forest canopy, he burst upon a man who was burying something with a shovel.

The man—an enormous bearded man in a black coat—let out a cry of surprise and terror, and pulled a revolver from under his coat. The gun was aimed squarely at Nathan.

"Captain Bim!" Nathan implored, guessing from the shape of him who it was.

The man's voice was trembling. "Young Mac-Allister?"

Nathan's eyes took in the dark shape of what appeared to be a small metal box that the trader had been burying. "Of course . . . it's just me. Am I glad it's *you*!"

Captain Bim put his revolver down. His voice thundered, "You took five years off my life!"

"I'm sorry. . . . You took ten off mine!"

"Young man, you just came within an eyelash of meeting your maker! What are you doing here?"

"I've been . . . exploring."

"Exploring! I thought I warned you to stay out of that forest."

Nathan's eyes went back to the box. A strongbox, that's what it was. He thought better of asking Captain Bim what *he* had been doing. "I think I found someone in a cave," he said instead. "Out at the Hole in the Wall."

The trader was dumbfounded. "You *think* you *found someone* in a *cave*? This is what you have to say for yourself?"

"At a little beach out near the tip of Cape Flattery. It's the survivor of the shipwreck. I mean, what if it is? What if it's the murderer! I saw a glint of light. It could have been from the knife that was stolen from your store."

"What exactly did you see?"

"Nothing exactly—it was so dark. Maybe two eyes. Maybe a man with a lot of hair and a beard. It was in a sea cave. I heard him for sure."

"What exactly did you hear?"

"Breathing. When he wasn't holding his breath. Oh, and I also saw lots of shells from mussels and clams that he'd been eating."

"Footprints?"

"The high tide had washed them away. Will you tell the Makahs tonight?"

With a laugh, the trader said, "Sounds like you've let your imagination run away with you!"

"What do you mean?"

"A lot of hair, and a beard, and some breathing . . . You've seen the Hairy Man! The Makahs will think you've seen the Hairy Man!"

"It's not a joke, Captain Bim! If you see Lighthouse George, will you tell him what I saw?"

"If you say so."

"I saw something else, too—a canoe up in a tree."

"I hope you didn't explore that."

After the briefest hesitation, Nathan said, "I told you, it was up in a tree."

"I call that a ghost canoe. There's a few of them tucked away here and there in the woods. That was an old burial you were looking at."

"Why would it be in a tree?"

"That's one of the ways the Makahs used to bury people, especially important ones. Probably there's the remains of a chief up in that canoe, and some of his personal effects for use in the afterlife."

"Do they still do that?" Nathan asked, trying to keep the big man talking.

"Nowadays they bury everyone in the ground— you've seen the village graveyard. Sometimes they build little spirit houses on top of the graves, so they can leave things for the deceased."

Nathan wished he could ask about the yellowed decorated bone cylinders in the small cedar box that had been left in the ghost canoe, but he couldn't without telling that he had indeed climbed into the tree and taken a look. He decided to keep asking questions, to try to lessen the tension that was still thick between him and the trader. Bim usually liked nothing better than talking. "What kind of stuff do they leave nowadays for the dead?"

"Dishes, baskets, maybe some tools," Bim said impatiently, waving him off. "You just stay clear away from any Makah graves, and especially stay away from that canoe, and any others like it. I won't tell Lighthouse George or anyone about that part of your explorations, and neither should you. Now get going, Young Mac. Your mother's probably given you up for dead."

Bim had managed to conceal the strongbox behind him, but he was still agitated. "And don't you say anything about our encounter this evening to anybody, ever, or I'll have your liver," Bim said, deadly serious. "Do you understand?"

"Yes, sir."

"What a headache you've given me! Go!"

Nathan took off at a run, anxious to get out from under the darkness of the trees and into the village.

What did Captain Bim have in that strongbox, and what was he doing out in the woods? As he hopped the village creek and passed alongside the great canoe that Young Carver had been shaping from a giant cedar log, Nathan made out the form of a man sleeping in the bottom of the canoe. His clothing was entirely dark except for a row of brass buttons down the middle of his jacket. The man sat up suddenly, frightening Nathan. His thin face was strange, scarred somehow. It was hard to see in the poor light.

"Dolla Bill," the man said, staring at Nathan and pointing at himself.

Nathan had never seen this Makah before. He was caught off guard, especially by the man's staring and his seemingly hollow eyes. A Makah had never asked him for money before. "I'm sorry," he said. "I don't have any money."

Nathan was surprised to hear the man ask, "Who are you?" in English. So few Makahs spoke any English.

"Nathan MacAllister," he replied.

"Poor Dolla Bill need a friend."

The man made no sense. Nathan wondered if there was something wrong with him. He had to get away from this man.

"I have to go," Nathan said, and he turned quickly for the cottage.

·8·
Dolla Bill

It seemed a night that would never end. Whichever way Nathan tossed and turned, he kept seeing that pair of eyes glimmering in the dark and the glint of the knife. He heard the breathing as vividly as if it were right there, in the front room of the cottage where he was pinned to his bed with fear. He wished he could tell his mind to quit remembering, but he couldn't. If only he could fall asleep. He'd never been so frightened in his life.

A second scene kept repeating itself: the terrified trader pulling out his revolver and pointing it straight at Nathan's heart. Fool that Bim was, Nathan realized, he might have pulled the trigger. Bim had come within an eyelash of shooting him. He'd said as much.

At last Nathan slept, perhaps for an hour or two. Then a dream in which he was surrounded by countless pairs of eyes, glowing in the dark, woke him up. With the first hint of dawn came a soft tapping at the cottage door. Nathan heard it from the front room and knew it was Lighthouse George. "Come now," George said.

The fisherman's shy smile was missing this morning. Nathan's eyes went immediately to the spear Lighthouse George was carrying, much taller than himself. It was lighter than the spear in the ghost canoe, and it branched into two fearsomely honed and barbed mussel-shell tips.

Nathan merely nodded and turned to get dressed as fast as he could. At his mother's door, he heard her coughing lightly. "Going with Lighthouse George," he whispered.

His mother was awake. "Rebecca says her husband thinks you will make a good fisherman."

"I hope so. Go back to sleep, Mother."

He didn't tell her that he thought they were going to be fishing for a man.

At the beach, in the improving light, a number of broad-shouldered Makah men were placing clubs and spears and paddles inside canoes about twenty-five feet in length—not their great canoes but not their smaller fishing canoes either. A war party, Nathan was certain of it. Captain Bim must have told Lighthouse George, who had told the rest of the Makahs about the man hiding in the cave out near the tip of Cape Flattery.

The morning star was shining bright over the Pacific. The clouds had passed through; the fog was gone. Nathan shivered in the cold as he watched

George and other men drop skid-poles every ten feet or so up the gravelly beach, all the way from the shore up to the canoes. Lighthouse George had motioned for him to stay on the porch of the trading post and wait. Now Nathan wondered if he was going along after all.

The Makahs began to skid their high-prowed canoes across the poles and down to the water. What if they found nothing out at the Hole in the Wall? What would they think of him?

Nathan noticed a man standing alone high on the beach, not working with the rest. It was the man who'd been sleeping in Young Carver's canoe. He was tall for a Makah, if he was a Makah, and unusually skinny. He was wearing a dark blue U.S. military jacket, which explained the brass buttons that had stood out in the dark.

A dog trotting along the beach on its early morning rounds approached the lone man, stopped and studied him, then steered away. Many Makahs over the age of twenty showed signs of having survived smallpox, but their faces hadn't been utterly ravaged by the disease, like this man's. He'd further disfigured his face with tattoos—circles with dots in their centers, two rows of them across his forehead. Yet it was his hollow eyes, even from a distance, that Nathan found the most disarming. Makahs never stared.

The strange man took off his military jacket, and then the shirt underneath, picked up a bunch of weeds he had apparently gathered, and began whipping his bare flesh with the weeds, on his chest and arms and back. At the same time he began a wailing chant that made Nathan's spine shiver. It sounded like the wailing of the damned, Nathan thought. Captain Bim, who was lumbering toward the trading post with his big key ring in his hand, barely paid attention to the eerie demonstration.

Bim had no greeting for Nathan other than a stiff nod. Nathan worried that the trader was angry with him.

"I'm sorry about last night—running into you like that," Nathan began.

"Not to be discussed," the trader said gruffly, "and we'll get along just fine."

The wailing from the pock-faced man continued, but the Makahs preparing the canoes paid him no attention.

"What's that he's thrashing himself with?" Nathan asked.

"Stinging nettles. The poor devil's going to suffer for that, and badly."

"But why's he doing it?"

"He wants to go with them."

"What's his name?"

"Dolla Bill, he says."

"Oh—I thought he wanted money."

"You met?"

"Sort of . . . last night. Is Dolla Bill his real name?"

"Of course not. Somebody gives them a name and it sticks."

"Where'd he come from?"

"He arrived with the *Anna Rose* yesterday from Port Townsend."

"That's not what I meant. He doesn't look like a Makah."

"He is and he isn't. He was a child here—in fact, he

remembered my name, after twenty years gone. Then I remembered him."

"Did his family remember him?"

"They're all dead, from smallpox, but they weren't his family to begin with. It used to be, all these tribes kept captives—slaves, essentially. They were treated well, but they were a chief's property all the same. When this man's Makah family died, some twenty years ago, another chief sold him and his sister to a British ship's captain. In fact, it was the year I first came, shortly after the big smallpox epidemic. Twenty-two years ago to be exact. The Makah were destitute. They'd lost over half their people to small-pox. One gold coin bought each child. I remember those children's faces—utterly forlorn—as they were led away. How could I forget?"

The trader spat, then added, "He shouldn't have bothered to come back here, but I suppose no place else looks like home."

"Where has he been?"

"All over the world, he says. But he won't fit back in so easily as Lighthouse George did. I remember what a big potlatch they gave when George returned. But Lighthouse George was the son of a *tyee*, a chief. He was born with the right to use the whaling harpoon, and you can't be born any higher in Makah society than that."

"I thought Lighthouse George became a harpooner on a whaleship, when he was away."

"They took him for a harpooner because he was already a master at it."

Nathan was thoroughly confused. "You're telling me that the Makahs hunt *whales*?"

The trader looked at him like there was no conceivable way to account for his ignorance. "Where have you been, Young Mac? That's who the Makah are! They hunt the great gray whale, to be exact. They're the only whaling tribe in these United States, and it's likely they've been whaling here for a thousand years or more."

"But I never knew.... Do you mean they hunt whales from their *canoes*?"

"They hunt the leviathans of the deep, young man. Forty-ton gray whales."

Captain Bim's gaze, and then Nathan's, was drawn to an old Makah approaching them from the canoes. Nathan recognized him from his long white hair and the abalone-shell earrings as the old man who'd been stripping planks from the cedar tree the day before. "Here comes Jefferson," Captain Bim said. "He's the top chief."

Jefferson strode directly up to Nathan and said, *"Kloshe tumtum mika chako."*

Nathan turned to Captain Bim. " 'Welcome'? Is that what he said?"

" 'Good intentions you come,' to be exact. In other words, you're invited. Somehow or other, you got on his good side—"

Before Nathan could even thank the chief, Jefferson was striding away. Nathan ran straight toward Lighthouse George's canoe. George had a Makah paddle ready for him, decorated with a fanciful design that might have represented an eagle. Nathan helped George and three other men launch the canoe. As soon as his feet hit the water, they hurt with the cold. He said nothing. He looked around at all the men in the canoes. This was a high honor. The youngest Makahs in the canoes were several years older than he was. He wondered if Lighthouse George had asked the chief to invite him along.

The next moment, he was helping to paddle a twenty-five-foot Makah canoe. He was seated on the last thwart toward the back.

Behind him, Lighthouse George was ruddering at the stern, and George already had the canoe pointed toward Koitlah Point at the northwestern end of Neah Bay. George began to chant in Makah, and the men answered him with a high-pitched song that served to keep all the paddles stroking in unison. Nathan made his strokes count, and the canoe shot forward on the water, fast as a killer whale.

As they were rounding Koitlah Point, Nathan glanced back at Neah Bay and saw a single canoe trailing them. One man was chasing them, paddling a small fishing canoe as fast as he could. Nathan could make out the blue military suit with the brass buttons. It was Dolla Bill.

·9·
Swims Like a Fish

Abruptly, the men in the lead canoe stopped paddling, and those in the other three canoes immediately quit singing and paddling as well. The forward motion of Lighthouse George's canoe brought it close enough for Nathan to see what was happening. The bowman in the lead canoe, with a motion of his thumb, was pointing in the direction of the Chibahdehl Rocks, where the *Burnaby* had foundered. Nathan spotted several large fur seals offshore of the rocks, afloat and sleeping on their backs.

The lead canoe went on alone. The Makahs' tapered paddles parted the water soundlessly. The canoe approached the seals as invisibly as the wind. The bowman stood slowly, brandishing a two-pointed spear like George's with rope attached. It was actually a harpoon, Nathan realized.

The bowman was nearly on the seals before they woke with a snort and a commotion. It was too late for one of them. The harpoon was thrown with deadly force and accuracy—the seal died almost instantly, pierced through the heart or lungs. On impact, the killing heads had detached from the weapon's shaft.

The canoes all paddled close as the men of the first canoe hauled on the rope and retrieved the huge animal. The seal was so heavy it had to be gutted before it could be hauled into the canoe.

Once again, paddles were flashing, including Nathan's. The canoes raced forward past Slant Rock and Mushroom Rock, both covered with cormorants and gulls. All the men were singing. Once they'd arrived at the tip of the Cape, Nathan was surprised that the canoes in front made no effort to weave a way among the seastacks hiding the Hole in the Wall, where he'd encountered the man in the cave. Instead, they remained out in the Strait. The canoes navigated easily around Jones Rock, between the Cape and Tatoosh, and began to turn south.

Fuca's Pillar was coming into sight. Nathan glanced back at Lighthouse George, for explanation, but an explanation wasn't forthcoming. The Makahs had left off singing once again, and their paddles parting the water made not a sound. The concentration of every man was so intense that Nathan left off paddling altogether, for fear he'd make a mistake. All he could hear was the surf and sea parrots by the hundreds beating their wings as they flew in and out of their nests in the cliffs.

Around the tip of the Cape, halfway down to Fuca's

Pillar, the canoes skirted a reef and aimed toward one of the many caves that the sea had carved into the mainland. Its mouth was perhaps twenty feet across. The canoes paused a hundred feet offshore, keeping their position. All eyes were on the cave. Nathan glanced to Lighthouse George. With his thumb, George motioned several times toward the cave.

Nathan concluded that his cave ran through the tip of Cape Flattery and connected back to the Hole in the Wall. The Makahs intended to sneak up on the fugitive by way of this cave. He wouldn't be able to escape up the stairs or by any other route.

The Makahs should have brought their smaller fishing canoes, Nathan thought. The twenty-five-foot canoes seemed large for maneuvering inside a cave.

To Nathan's surprise some of the Makahs in every canoe, including Lighthouse George, began to remove their shirts and trousers. They stripped down to their shorts, and then they began to tie their long hair into topknots. From a cedar box, one of the men in Nathan's canoe produced dozens of sticks whittled from some sort of pitchwood; Nathan handed a bunch back to Lighthouse George, as he was directed. Another man brought out a clam shell and gently opened it up. A live coal was glowing inside.

The first man to take the clam shell lit one stick at a time, placed them upright in his hair, and passed the coal on. In every canoe, men were doing the same. The paddlers who hadn't stripped were guiding the canoes soundlessly closer to the cave entrance. All the while, none of them spoke a word.

The coal came to Lighthouse George, who lit the sticks and placed them flaming upright in his hair.

George made a swimming motion with his arms. For the first time Nathan understood that the men meant to swim into the cave.

The swimmers began to slip over the sides of the canoes. Lighthouse George was about to join them. Nathan pointed to himself and then to the cave entrance, and made the swimming motion himself. "Good swimmer," he mouthed, and he began to take off his clothes. *"Mamook swim kloshe,"* he whispered to the surprised Makah in front of him in the canoe.

Lighthouse George nodded, then put his fingers to his lips. Nathan nodded in return, showing he understood the need for utter silence.

The shock of the Pacific's frigid water set his heart pounding as he lowered himself over the side of the canoe. Two of the swimmers were being handed short clubs carved in the image of seals, like the one he had seen in the ghost canoe. Lighthouse George was handed a neat coil of rope such as Nathan had seen Rebecca braiding from strips of the inner bark of cedar. Nathan was not disappointed that the men staying behind in the canoe gave him nothing to carry, leaving his hands free.

The swimmers from the other canoes were already approaching the mouth of the cave. Nathan began to breaststroke toward it, alongside Lighthouse George, who was keeping a close watch on him to see if he was as strong a swimmer as he'd claimed.

He was. He'd swum in the surf with his father along carefully selected spots on the California coast. He knew the power of the surf. He knew to go with it and never to fight it, especially if he was ever caught in a riptide and swept out to sea.

As Nathan was about to enter the mouth of the cave, he had to adjust suddenly as a wave surged and almost threw him against the cliff. With several strong strokes he was into the cave mouth alongside Lighthouse George. The water was cold, so cold! With relief, he could see that the cave was lit up brightly by all the flaming pitch-sticks crowning the heads of the swimmers in front of them.

A passage of no more than thirty feet led to a grotto perhaps fifty feet across and thirty feet high. It was eerie how quietly all the men were swimming. Neither hands nor feet were breaking the surface. The swimmers were fanning out now all along the width of the brightly lit grotto. Nathan couldn't see another tunnel leading out. He was confused. It couldn't possibly connect to the Hole in the Wall.

There were smooth, rounded shapes all over a rock shelf that spanned the rear of the cave. Seals, Nathan realized, as they began to lift their heads. Hair seals, quite a bit smaller than the great fur seal. He could see at least fifty pairs of eyes shining.

All the Makahs, and Nathan too, swam to within feet of the rock shelf and the seals. He could see the whiskered faces of the seals clear as day, but the seals apparently couldn't see him. They were blinded, he realized. Blinded by the light. For the first time he realized that he was on a seal-hunting, and not a man-hunting, expedition.

Perhaps someone had given a signal. The men with the clubs slipped out of the water all in one fluid motion. And in the next moment, swiftly and surely, they were cracking the skulls of the seals.

Barely more than half of the seals escaped. Nathan felt the turbulence in the water from one that exploded past him in its desperate flight from the cave.

"Lotsa meat, lotsa oil," Lighthouse George said as they paddled for home. Nathan wondered if this would be a good time to tell George about seeing the fugitive in the cave. Obviously, Bim hadn't. He wondered if George would say once again that it wasn't the Makahs' business, and he worried that George might be upset at hearing about him going off alone and doing something so dangerous.

Nonetheless, he had to get the word out that there was someone hiding at the Cape. Just as he was about to speak, all the Makahs stopped paddling. They were staring at a man marooned on one of the smaller rocks that stood among the giant seastacks offshore of the Hole in the Wall. It was Dolla Bill.

Lighthouse George motioned for his paddlers to rescue the man. The surf buffeting the rock and the weight of the dead seals in the canoe tested George's skill at the rudder position, but he was able to bring the canoe close enough for Dolla Bill to spring into the center of the canoe among the seals.

The pock-faced, tattooed outcast began speaking wildly in a combination of Makah, Chinook, and English, waving his arms all the while. His canoe, he claimed, had been stolen by a "hairy white *skookumman*" who was "strong as ten men" and "swims like a fish."

Now Nathan knew he had to tell George what he'd seen. But he would wait for a better time, not in front of a crazy man.

On arriving at Neah Bay, Lighthouse George did something surprising. Unlike the rest of the Makah, who were ignoring Dolla Bill, Lighthouse George took the outcast to his longhouse, which he shared with four other families. With Nathan at his side, George designated a place by his and Rebecca's corner where Dolla Bill would sleep. Nathan saw Lighthouse George point to Rebecca's fire pit and say something in Makah. Nathan realized that George was saying that this was the place where Dolla Bill would eat. They were going to feed him.

The outcast broke into tears and threw himself at George's feet. George spoke sharply, and Dolla Bill stood, forcing himself to regain what little dignity he possessed. Like Lighthouse George, he pretended that nothing had happened.

·10·
Yaw-ka-duke

"Hairy white *skookum-man*." The phrase kept repeating itself in the back of Nathan's mind as he paddled past the Hole in the Wall the next morning with Lighthouse George. Nathan craned for a glimpse, perhaps, of the tip of the stolen canoe behind the rocks, but he saw nothing.

He kept paddling, around the tip of the Cape, past the cave of the seals, past Fuca's Pillar. They were headed for the halibut banks. He and George were going fishing.

Nathan decided it was time to broach the subject of the fugitive with Lighthouse George. "Do you believe Dolla Bill, about what he saw?"

"Dolla Bill doesn't lie to me," George replied. "He knows that I can see the part of him that is still good. I understand how he let all the hurt of the world poi-

81

son him during the years that he was away. But he has a little bit of hope that he won't always be this way. And so I try to help him."

"I think I saw the same man Dolla Bill saw," Nathan said, and then he told his story of what had happened at the Hole in the Wall.

George listened with a grave expression all the way through, and then said, "*Hyas cultus*. This is bad."

"What I saw was barely a shadow. Dolla Bill saw him in broad daylight. Is there any way to prove that Dolla Bill was telling the truth?"

"The marshal will come again from Port Townsend. The agent sent for him. The marshal will find out."

"Good," Nathan said.

He thought of how frightened Dolla Bill had been by what he had seen, and how frightened he himself had been. Who, or what, was this man?

He said to George, "I know *skookum* means 'powerful.' But the way Dolla Bill said it, *skookum-man* must mean more than just strong. Dolla Bill's eyes were as big as silver dollars—it looked to me like he'd seen a ghost."

"It means that, too," George replied, without missing a stroke. "Or an evil spirit, or a demon. But it's not good to talk of such things. Evil can hear its name called."

When they reached the fishing spot that George had decided upon, under towering cliffs, they sank bentwood hooks to the sea bottom on long lines Rebecca had woven from three strands of inner cedar bark. "From the size of these lines," Nathan said, "halibut must be pretty big fish."

"Great One Coming Against the Current," the fisherman replied with a smile.

The U-shaped wooden hooks were as big as Nathan's hand. He and George had baited the bone barbs with octopus—six sets altogether. The hooks were designed to float a foot or two off the bottom, where they were attached to a stone sinker by a slipknot. On the surface of the ocean, the lines were tied to wooden floats carved in the images of sea otters floating on their backs.

After a short wait, one of the wooden floats on the surface came suddenly to life. Nathan wanted to paddle directly to the buoy and pull hard on the line, but George said, "Not yet, *Yaw-ka-duke*. Let Rises Steeply eat some more."

The first halibut was so large that when they hauled it to the surface, its thrashing threatened to damage or even upset the canoe. At last George was able to thrust a long, sharpened pole through the gills of the enormous white fish with eyes on top of its head. With the pole over one knee and under the other, George lifted the great flatfish and dealt it a swift death blow with his club.

Nathan forgot to ask George what *Yaw-ka-duke* meant. When they reached Neah Bay, and he was on his way back to the cottage, he asked Captain Bim, who didn't know. "Must be a Makah word," the trader muttered. The trader was still out of sorts. Two days had passed, but it seemed Bim wasn't going to forgive being surprised with the shovel and the strongbox. If anything, he seemed more and more perturbed. What did Captain Bim have in the box that made him act so strange about it? Was it money, or was it something else? Had he found some of that Spanish treasure?

"I heard the territorial marshal is coming," Nathan ventured.

"*If* your wild man ever existed," the trader snorted, "he'd be long gone by now."

"What do you mean by '*if*'? Do you mean you still don't believe—"

"Consider the sources," Bim interrupted haughtily. "A former slave who is patently insane and an impressionable boy who frightened himself in a cave."

Nathan left the trading post fuming. Bim would cut off his own nose to spite his face!

As he approached the cottage and smelled the comforting aroma of fresh baking, Nathan put the disagreeable meeting with the trader behind him. Rebecca was coming out through the screen door with a basketful of fresh bread for the longhouse. As always, she had a warm smile for Nathan. "Good fishing?" she asked.

"We could've sunk the boat," he replied proudly. "Lotsa halibut."

"*Klo-she*. I go take care of them."

"What's *Yaw-ka-duke* mean?" Nathan remembered to ask.

"Sort of like 'friend.' 'Partner,' that's what you call it."

"*Yaw-ka-duke*," Nathan whispered, proud and pleased.

The next day, when they delivered the mail out to Tatoosh, he brought a prime halibut to his father and told him all about the fishing. He also told his father about the *skookum-man*. Nathan's father listened solemnly to his son's account of going down the ancient stairs and detecting the man in the sea cave, and then he listened as Nathan told Dolla Bill's story of the theft of the canoe. When Nathan was finished, his father's gray eyes turned inward, and he remained silent, deeply troubled.

"George believes Dolla Bill was telling the truth," Nathan added.

"Then I do as well," Zachary MacAllister said. "I'm displeased that you went out to the Cape alone. That was hardly prudent. At least we can assume that this man has fled the area, now that he has a canoe."

Nathan left Tatoosh without telling his father about Captain Bim's strongbox. He feared that telling Bim's secret might mean risking his life, or even his father's. Nathan remembered the barrel of the revolver too well, and Captain Bim's words: "Don't you say anything about our encounter . . . or I'll have your liver." Bim had meant it.

He hated keeping secrets from his father, but now he had two, and temperamental Captain Bim knew them both: the buried strongbox and the ancient canoe he'd discovered up in the tree. Nathan knew he dare not tell anyone about the ghost canoe, not after what Captain Bim had told him. The Makahs would be very upset with him, especially if they learned he'd climbed up and looked at the burial, even touched things—maybe Lighthouse George wouldn't want him around anymore.

Over the next two days, Nathan and George filled the fishing canoe to capacity again. All the Makah fishermen were doing well. With all the thin-sliced halibut on the drying racks, Neah Bay, from a distance, looked as if it were decorated with thousands of white flags.

At last the territorial marshal came. Unfortunately, he came and went while Nathan was out fishing. "It was just as I said it would be," Captain Bim reported smugly. "Once the marshal took a look at the sole eyewitness, Dolla Bill, all he wanted was to get back to Port Townsend as quickly as possible. It was much easier to believe that Dolla Bill had wrecked the canoe or stolen it for himself."

"Didn't he even go out to the Hole in the Wall and search?"

"He spent several hours out there. He didn't find anything."

"I never got a chance to tell him what I saw. Did you tell him?"

"Aye, I mentioned that, and I mentioned that some Makah children had also seen the Hairy Man in the woods, too. The marshal didn't appear to be impressed. Look, young man, I've been here over twenty years. Neah Bay is not so exciting as your imaginings would have it."

"So nothing's going to happen," Nathan said sadly. "He's going to get away—probably get away with murder."

The trader paused. "*If* you're right about all this, Young Mac, there's nothing to be done in any event. Your fugitive would have paddled to one of the ports on the Canadian side, that would be my bet, and by now he would be beyond the reach of the law."

·11·
Stolen Dreams

Captain Bim took Dolla Bill on as a second assistant in the store, which surprised Nathan and made him consider the possibility that both of them, along with the fugitive, had been involved in some grand conspiracy. But then he rejected the idea, because there was a much simpler explanation for the hiring of the outcast. Dolla Bill spoke English, and having him in the store gave the trader someone to talk to all day long. For Bim, that was reason enough. And Dolla Bill, now an employee in the store, was beginning to act almost normal.

One day, while Nathan was at the trading post, a sudden commotion erupted down on the beach. People were shouting and running every which way in what looked like a tidal wave of excitement.

"What's happening?" Nathan asked.

"Eulachon," Captain Bim explained as he stood on the porch of the trading post and surveyed the activity on the beach. "They're late this year."

"Who are eulachon?" Nathan ventured.

"They're not a 'who,' Young Mac. They're fish—small, silver fish," the trader replied irritably. "Also known as candlefish, the 'fish that burns.' They're eaten fresh, dried for food, or rendered for *glease*."

"Do you mean grease?"

"Of course I mean grease, young man. Do you object if I pepper my speech with Chinook?"

"I'm sorry," Nathan said. Nothing he could say turned out right with Captain Bim anymore. "I just wanted to make sure—I couldn't see how you could get grease from a fish."

"Well, you can. It's immensely valuable among all the tribes. They slather it all over the fish they're eating, and almost anything else. Only a few of the tribes control the trade. The grease trails—those are trading routes—go clear into the remote interior of Canada."

Nathan was about to turn and go. He knew Lighthouse George would be going after the eulachon if they were so important, and could use his help. Suddenly Nathan felt the pressure of the big man's hand on his shoulder. He looked back and saw anguish in the trader's bloodshot eyes.

"Why do you torment me?" Bim asked, his voice tense and unnatural.

"I—I don't understand," Nathan stammered.

"You take me for a fool. I know when I'm being spied upon."

Nathan protested his innocence. He had no idea what Bim was talking about, and asked him to explain. But the trader would say no more, and Nathan could tell Bim hadn't believed him.

Perplexed, Nathan turned and ran down toward the beach. Spying? What could Bim have meant? Nathan was happy to find Lighthouse George on the beach, and added his shoulder to those of four men who helped George portage his canoe over to the swamp behind the village, where the Waatch River began its short run to the Pacific.

The two of them, along with Makahs in dozens of other fishing canoes, paddled down the gentle river toward the sea. At the river's mouth, where it flowed into the Pacific at Makah Bay, hundreds of Makahs assembled to take as many of the seething eulachon as they might. Some people set out bag nets in the shallows while others, like Nathan and George, fished from their canoes with dip nets.

The smeltlike eulachon drifted in from the Pacific in teeming schools. Sea lions and porpoises followed them right into the shallow river. Screaming hordes of seagulls filled the air, diving to snatch the silvery fish, and bald eagles skimmed the water and raked sometimes two or three at once in their talons. Nathan saw, offshore, the tall dorsal fins of killer whales, who must have been taking their considerable share—unless it was the sea lions and the porpoises they were hunting. Lighthouse George had told him that the killer whales worked in packs, just like wolves. There is a story, George explained, that in the early times killer whales had actually been land wolves. Now they are wolves of the sea.

The eulachon run lasted three days. The crows, the ravens, and the eagles glutted themselves on spawned-out, dead eulachon washed up all along the banks of the river.

The Makahs ate some of their eulachon fresh, and they dried it and smoked it, but most of it they buried in pits lined and covered with logs. When the fish were thoroughly rotten ten days later, the entire disintegrated mass was heated in large cedar boxes or else in canoes such as Lighthouse George's.

When the time came to render the grease, Nathan helped George and Rebecca. Trying to ignore the stench as best he could, he brought dozens of red-hot stones on forked carrying sticks from the fire to the canoe and dropped them inside. The stones had to be retrieved and reheated again and again. Rebecca, with her big cedar ladle, skimmed the grease from the top by the gallon and stored it in bentwood cedar boxes decorated with elaborate carvings. One of the designs depicted a gigantic creature that was part man and part bird—the same figure Nathan had seen on the prow of the ghost canoe. Its wings were spread wide, and it was clutching an entire whale in its talons.

Lighthouse George was pleased. "Lotsa fish oil, lotsa seal oil for the potlatch," he told Nathan. "The Nitinats are coming soon from Vancouver Island for a big potlatch. Last time we paddled over there, we got lotsa gifts. Now it's our turn."

Nathan was on his way to the cottage, bringing a small box of the eulachon grease from Rebecca as a gift to his mother. Rebecca said to try dipping clams or fish or almost anything in it. As Nathan passed close to the trading post, he was hailed by a trembling voice.

It was Captain Bim, like a wounded bear, all in a rage.

The big man ordered him inside. "What's the matter?" Nathan ventured, stepping into the trading post. It was late in the evening—a terrifying conclusion to a seemingly endless and perfect June day. The trading post was closed, and there was no one else around. It was too dark to see clearly. Once Captain Bim was inside, his rage suddenly turned to tears. He shuddered with huge uncontrollable sobs.

"What's the matter?" Nathan repeated. He had never seen a grown man break down, but this man was broken.

"My money box! It's gone! It's all I have in the world."

"Captain Bim . . . ," Nathan pleaded. "I don't know what you're talking about!"

The trader tore at his beard. "It was my dream! I was going to open a little ice-cream parlor in Port Townsend, just like the ones they have in San Francisco. I was going to build a home on the hill, where I could watch the ships come and go. It took me twenty-two years to save the money in that box, and I did it honestly, by God."

"But Captain Bim," Nathan protested. "I didn't take it! Please believe me! I didn't even know what it was you were burying. I . . . I thought you might have found some of that Spanish gold you told me about! I never told a soul, just like you said."

"How did you know it was gold?"

"I didn't! I didn't have any idea what was in there!"

Bim glared at him, and then snarled, "Gold it was, but hardly Spanish treasure. Twenty-dollar gold pieces, that's what was in the box, my life's savings, but I suppose you already know that, and have counted them out!"

"I don't know anything!"

"You say you haven't told a soul, Red? More likely you haven't told a soul where you put it. Is that what you meant?"

"Haven't told a soul that I ever ran into you that night and saw that box!"

"You're telling me it wasn't you who took it today?"

"I swear, Captain Bim—it wasn't me!"

The trader gasped for air, and then took several more deep breaths. He stared long and hard into Nathan's eyes, and then he seemed calmer. "I want to believe you. . . . You always seemed like a decent fellow, of upstanding stock. . . . But who, then?"

"I don't know. I really don't know!"

"I suppose it could have been Dolla Bill. I've been wondering if he's been stealing from the store, and I suspect he has. I suppose he's been skulking around in the dark and saw me moving the box. It's my own fault for drawing so much attention to myself. Ever since that time you surprised me, I've moved it every night! I was just so afraid, and I knew someone was watching me. I could feel it! Sometimes I moved it twice in one night!"

"No wonder you've been so tired. Are any of the coins marked? Dolla Bill might spend one."

"No, they're not marked!" the trader bellowed. "Clever boy, you always have a suggestion, don't you?"

Nathan saw the rage suddenly return to the trader's face, and he knew the man was deadly serious. He saw the shape of the revolver as Captain Bim took it from inside his coat. It was pointed at Nathan's heart.

"Trying to throw the blame onto that pathetic outcast . . . You're a clever liar, boy! You're the one who saw the box! Swear on your mother's soul, Red, that it wasn't you. Swear she'll be damned for eternity if you're lying."

Nathan swore, in a calm voice, on his mother's soul.

To his relief, Captain Bim believed him.

The trader collapsed on a chair. He took off his cap and crushed it between his hands. "Keep your friends close, and your enemies closer, they always say. I'll watch Dolla Bill like a hawk! I'll have his liver!"

"I'm sorry this happened to you, Captain Bim. I feel awful."

"I'm lost now, Young Mac. If it had been you, I'd have had a chance of getting it back."

"Tell the territorial marshal."

"I can't. I'm going to have to sell the trading post. If news of this got out, it would cripple my bargaining position. People would think me desperate. Promise you won't tell."

"I promise."

Nathan had another secret to keep.

·12·
The Arrival of the Nitinats

Nathan was sitting on the front stoop of the cottage, looking out to sea, when he first saw them, far off in the waters of the Strait. He studied the shimmering shapes, trying to figure out what they could be. For a long time they appeared to be sea serpents, twenty or more sea serpents lifting their tall heads above the waters.

They were nearing Neah Bay, very gradually nearing. Suddenly he recognized them for what they were—high-prowed, very large canoes. Then he remembered that this was the day that the Makahs' distant relations from the west coast of Vancouver Island were arriving for the big potlatch. Jefferson was celebrating an event in his family; a marriage, Nathan thought it was.

Even from a mile away, Nathan could see that large

numbers of Makahs were gathering on the beach to welcome the Nitinats. He called to his mother, and she came out of the cottage to watch the flotilla of canoes approaching. "Let's go see the welcome together," she said.

It proved a pageant Nathan would never forget. Long before any faces were visible in the canoes, there came the beat of drums across the water, to which the Makah responded in kind. At last the two canoes in the lead, and their occupants, began to take shape. Dancing on a plank across the gunwales just behind the prow of one canoe, a grizzly bear was raking the air with one paw and then the next. "Surely it's a man inside a bear skin," Elizabeth MacAllister whispered, but the deception was so complete that Nathan had to wonder for a moment.

A man-sized raven with a bill nearly three feet long was dancing at the prow of the other lead canoe. Wings, shaggy throat feathers, and body feathers completed the mischievous caricature suggested by the carved black mask.

From the corner of his eye, Nathan noticed that Bim, at the rear of the crowd on the beach, was watching as well. Earlier in the summer, Nathan would have gone to him to hear his comments. Nearly two weeks had passed since Bim had accused him of stealing all his money, and still it was difficult to be around the trader. They both knew they were avoiding each other; the feelings between them were much too strong. He hadn't even asked Bim what he thought when the Makahs reported another fishing canoe missing just two days after Bim's money was stolen.

As the high-prowed canoes of the visitors hovered

on the swell just outside the breaking waves, the Makahs sang a welcome song. The visitors responded by removing their paddles from the water and resting them upright on the gunwales of the canoes, blades in the air. There were no fishing canoes here; these were the great canoes, every one. Each canoe carried upward of fifteen men, women, and children.

Holding a carved staff, a white-haired chief at the stern of the grizzly canoe stood and made a speech, which was answered by one from the *hyas tyee* of the Makahs, old Jefferson, who was clutching a similar emblem of his office.

As soon as the people disembarked and the canoes were unloaded and skidded above the high-tide line on the beach, a parade ensued, with the Makahs and their visitors walking up and down the beach in all their finery and singing. Like many of the women, Rebecca wore a dress fashioned from a red blanket and festooned with white buttons. Lighthouse George, in addition to a grand red cape, was wearing a three-piece suit with abalone buttons that matched the abalone earrings he wore for the occasion.

The parade was followed by canoe races to Waadah Island and back, with bets of jewelry and blankets being placed all during the race. Four canoes from each tribe, seven men pulling plus the rudder paddler, raced to Waadah Island and back. Dolla Bill had tried to enlist for each of the four Makah canoes, including Lighthouse George's, and had been turned down by every one. "Don't feel bad," Nathan told him as the race began.

"Poor Dolla Bill," he said. "Poor Dolla Bill. George

feed me, but George don't love me. Captain Bim, same, same."

Nathan knew that what Dolla Bill had said was true. But he wanted to console the outcast, even if he might be a thief. "I didn't even try to join George's canoe," Nathan said. "We're not as strong as those men—look at the size of their backs. George wants to win."

Dolla Bill's face contorted with anger. "Strong as two men!" he declared.

It occurred to Nathan that Dolla Bill should be acting differently in some way if he actually was in possession of a boxful of gold coins. If he really had all that money, wouldn't it show?

The outcast watched the entire race with keen attentiveness. Competition was fierce as the canoes neared the beach, and Dolla Bill took to jumping up and down like a frenzied dog on a short leash. It was a Makah canoe, though not George's, that won by a mere prow's length at the very last.

An announcement was made by one of the Makah chiefs, and everyone went streaming toward the carved doorposts of the Potlatch House, the largest of the longhouses. Nathan's mother, who was tired and heading home, suggested he go see what happened next, so he would be able to tell her all about it.

More people crammed inside the Potlatch House than Nathan would have thought humanly possible. Inside, a feast was laid out, with Makah delicacies including kelp leaves upon which herring had laid their eggs, octopus stew, and fermented salmon eggs that had the consistency of cheese. People washed down their meat and fish—dried, smoked, roasted, and boiled—with quantities of eulachon oil. For himself, Nathan gorged on pilot bread, which he lathered with blackstrap molasses.

When the people were done eating, everyone turned toward one end of the hall, where all manner of goods were arrayed beside Jefferson, who began to give them away to his guests: blankets, clothes, bentwood cedar boxes filled with eulachon oil and seal oil, baskets, cedar household implements, bows and arrows, harpoons, lengths of fishing and sealing line, halibut hooks, sealskins, bearskins, woven mats, carved totems, a barrel of raw sugar and one of molasses, plug tobacco . . . anything and everything.

Nathan stayed awake through the first dances of the mythical figures in carved and painted masks, but he didn't understand the stories the dances were telling, and he was no longer able to keep his eyelids apart. He was awakened much later by the excitement of the crowd. A man on the platform where the dancers had performed was twirling a musket around his body faster than the eye could see. Limber as a snake and all muscle, the man had shaved his head and painted his body a reddish yellow from the waist up. In the light of the longhouse torches, his body glowed as if on fire.

To the amazement of the crowd, the performer began to juggle three long-bladed knives. The juggler's eyes never followed the knives; they stared straight ahead all the while. Nathan recognized those eyes, and then the pockmarks showing from under the paint. It was Dolla Bill.

Setting two of the knives aside, Dolla Bill appeared to swallow the third, then drew it back out of his throat. His entire audience gasped in appreciation.

The outcast had become the center of attention, glorying in it, and he was only getting started. Dolla Bill shattered a piece of glass, then ate it, after which he drew an endless stream of paper out of his mouth. He rolled a cannonball around his shoulders and along his arms, as if it weighed nothing. Returning to the stage, he ended the night by eating fire from one of the longhouse torches, then breathing it back out as a dragon might, in an explosive burst of flame.

"*Skookum-man,*" people were whispering as they left the Potlatch House.

"Obviously," Bim explained, "Dolla Bill has worked in Barnum's circus somewhere. But I've never seen the equal of his performance. He truly is a *skookum-man,* a demon as well as a thief.*"

Nathan was reminded of another *skookum-man.* "Strong as ten men," Dolla Bill had described the phantom. "Swims like a fish." What had become of him?

He'd paddled away, Nathan had to concede, escaped by sea. Now he would never be able to prove the fugitive really existed, that the phantom hadn't been, as everyone said, a product of his imagination.

·13·
The Bone Game

Around noon on the second day of the potlatch, the *Anna Rose* appeared offshore on its weekly rounds. Nathan barely noticed the canoes paddling out to meet the steamer and returning. He was absorbed with the progress of a gambling game between the Makahs and the Nitinats that was being played on the beach above the high-tide line.

A line of Makah men was sitting cross-legged opposite a line of Nitinat men, with about twenty feet separating the opposing players. Lighthouse George had a bone cylinder hidden in each of his hands, virtually identical to the ones Nathan had seen in the small cedar box in the ghost canoe. One cylinder had a band of black around its middle, while the other was unmarked. Nathan had determined that the object of the game was to guess which hand hid the unmarked bone. The bone handler's team—at this moment the Makahs—did everything in their power to make the guessing as difficult as possible.

As Lighthouse George moved his arms in a wild figure-eight pattern, sometimes tossing a bone in the air and sometimes perhaps exchanging bones between his hands, his team members were making a tremendous racket. They pounded on hand drums and beat sticks on a long board laid in front of them. In addition to making so much noise, the Makah team was chanting, and their wild chant was joined by all the Makahs standing behind them. The effect, as the minutes went by, was a rising, confusing, unbearable tide of pressure directed at the guesser. Sometimes as much as ten minutes went by before the guesser from the opposing team thought he was sure, and hazarded his guess. Nathan had been watching since morning. They called the game *sla hal.*

Now he knew why the bones had been placed in the ghost canoe. In addition to his hunting weapons, as he paddled into eternity, the chief would need his gambling bones for playing *sla hal.*

More and more goods had been added to the wagered pile between the two sides, until it had become a sizable heap. It seemed an opportunity for the Makahs to win back a small portion of all that Jefferson had given away the night before, but that didn't seem likely. The way the game worked, if the guesser guessed right, the bones were turned over to his team. An incorrect guess, and the guesser's team had to hand over a counter stick to the opposition. The game had started hours before, and the Nitinats had won all but two of the twenty counter sticks.

The Makahs had nearly been defeated, but Nathan was confident that Lighthouse George would turn the tide.

Suddenly the Nitinat guesser extended his left hand, signaling his guess. In an instant, all the drumming, pounding, and chanting from the Makah side ceased. George's face told it all—he opened the fingers of his left hand to reveal the unmarked bone. He had failed to win a counter back for his side, and the bones were going over to a new Nitinat handler.

Now it was the Nitinats' turn to handle the bones, to pound their sticks on their board, to chant and drum and create confusion, and it was Lighthouse George's turn to guess for the Makahs.

When the moment came, after only three or four minutes, Lighthouse George threw out his right hand, and his guess proved correct.

The bones came to the next Makah, who was Dolla Bill. Nathan wondered why the Makahs had included him in the game, but then recalled the sleight of hand Dolla Bill had demonstrated the night before.

The outcast closed his fingers on the bones, and then his hands, arms, and elbows went flying, weaving a pattern in and out that seemed a blur, it was done so fast. The Makahs beat harder than ever on the board in front of them and chanted louder than ever. The guesser, incapable of keeping up with Dolla Bill's hands, tried to read his eyes. But his eyes stared straight ahead, as they had the night before when he was juggling the knives. Empty of expression, his eyes told nothing.

Finally the Nitinat guesser threw out his left hand,

and Dolla Bill stopped instantly. As he uncurled the fingers of his own left hand, the black band of the marked bone was revealed, to the delight of the Makahs and the dismay of their guests.

A counter stick came over, and soon a second and a third and a fourth. The spectators kept looking at each other, wondering how long Dolla Bill's streak could last. Nathan looked up during the height of the noise and confusion and the feints and the flailing of the tattooed man's arms, and he noticed a white man was watching, a man he had never seen before. Nathan realized that the man must have arrived with the *Anna Rose*—one of the occasional tourists that the steamer brought to Neah Bay, from the looks of him. He was a natty dresser, sporting a straw Panama hat, a white suit, and white shoes.

Nathan guessed the visitor to be ten years younger than his father. His rugged face seemed to have been similarly sculpted by the elements, appearing at odds with the gentleman's apparel he was wearing. What struck Nathan most was the intensity of the man's eyes, piercingly blue, the bluest he had ever seen. Those blue eyes were locked on Dolla Bill, as were everyone's. A grin was playing at the man's lips. Nathan wasn't surprised to see Captain Bim sidle over to the stranger's side and strike up a conversation. The Makah's clamor reached a fever pitch, and the Nitinat guesser made his guess. Wrong again, and another counter went over.

Into the afternoon the game continued, with more and more goods being wagered by the Makahs as the counters went over to their side one by one. Dolla Bill seemed somehow to have achieved a plateau of invincibility. It seemed that no one on either side really believed that he could be outguessed.

The Makahs now owned all the counters but one. The excitement was unbearable. The last guesser made his guess—wrong—and the last counter came over to the Makahs. From the crowd's reaction, Nathan could tell that no one had ever seen such a winning streak at *sla hal.* "*Skookum-man,*" people were saying. "*Skookum-Bill.*"

Even though Dolla Bill was their champion, the Makahs still avoided him afterward. At the trading post, where they had no choice but to come face to face with him, they averted their eyes and skittered away quickly once they'd done business with him. Nathan felt the same way. Even a glance at Bill's eyes was unnerving.

A second feast was held that night in the Potlatch House, and Jefferson gave away as many gifts as he had the night before. Captain Bim brought the gentleman tourist to witness the spectacle. They were close enough that Nathan could hear bits and pieces of their conversation, which was almost completely one-sided. From what Nathan could gather, Bim was trying to interest the visitor in buying the trading post. At the same time, he was extolling the charms of Neah Bay and the Makah nation.

The man in the white suit seemed bored by all the giving, which went on and on, and he was bored by the dances. But when Dolla Bill was brought back to the platform for a repeat performance of the act he'd done the evening before, the visitor came to life and watched with intense concentration. Everyone did.

The grin that Nathan had seen at the bone game reappeared on the man's lips and remained there until Dolla Bill had left the platform.

During the third day of potlatch, Nathan brought a basket of pastries to the trading post. His mother had baked them for Captain Bim, to try to improve his melancholy spirits.

"Come in, come in," Bim cried, in surprisingly good humor, as Nathan tried to hand the basket through the door. "Sit down and have coffee with us."

Nathan was introduced to the man in the white suit, who sat at the table. They shook hands. The visitor's name was Jack Kane. He was a strikingly handsome man with a rugged, clean-shaven, weathered face under wavy blond hair. "I'm very pleased to meet you," Kane said warmly. His handshake was mild, though self-assured, like his voice. Nathan thought that this man might be easier to be around than the moody and unpredictable Captain Bim.

The stranger flashed a smile. "So you're the young man Captain Bim has been telling me about—the son of the lighthouse keeper."

Nathan was putting a third spoonful of sugar in his coffee. "Yes, sir. I hope he didn't tell you anything too bad."

"By no means," the blue-eyed Kane replied. "He says I'd be lucky to have you work in the store—if I bought the business, that is."

"You're considering it?"

"Considering, yes."

"Where are you from?" As soon as Nathan had asked, he glanced at Bim, wondering if it was something he shouldn't have said. He didn't want to hurt

Bim's delicate negotiations. He saw no signal from the trader.

"San Francisco. Would you indeed work in the store?"

"Sorry," Nathan said quickly. "I'm Lighthouse George's fishing partner. And to tell you the truth, I can't stand to be cooped up."

Kane laughed. "I feel much the same way. But I expect I'll find plenty of opportunities to lead the outdoor life in Neah Bay."

"I had recommended that Mr. Kane find a replacement for Dolla Bill," Bim explained. "Bill is a performer, not a clerk."

A smile came to the visitor's face. "Dolla Bill fascinates me. A remarkable performer, really."

"He keeps on winning at *sla hal*," Nathan said. "I'm going to watch some more this morning."

"The bone game intrigues me as well. The pieces have a charm to them—works of art, really."

Nathan drank down the rest of his coffee fast. "Well, I have to get going!"

Captain Bim nodded his head in approval. Nathan shook hands with the prospective buyer and left wondering how the trader was faring with his negotiations. Nathan hoped Kane was serious and would stay in Neah Bay.

The potlatch continued for a third day, and a fourth, until Jefferson had given away everything he had, including his canoe and his paddle, his clothes, and nearly a thousand dollars in gold and silver coin. Nathan's mother said that the Indian agent was furious. "We can teach them to operate sewing machines and we can teach them carpentry and mechanics until the

cows come home," he had told her, "but until we out-
law potlatch, they'll never progress. They need to
learn the importance of private property. How can
they ever get ahead as long as they'll give away their
wealth to enhance their honor?"

"It's like Christmas," his mother had suggested.
"And from what I understand, the Nitinats will host
the Makahs and do all the giving next time."

The agent, whom she didn't especially like, had
been cross with her. "It's barbarous," he'd insisted.
"All that will have to go, along with the longhouses
and the smokehouses and all the rest of it. Completely
unsanitary—the fishing, the sealing, the whaling, and
all the rest. We need to teach them a whole different
way of life. They need to be farmers."

"I hope they're better farmers than I," his mother
had told the agent. "With the poor soil, the wind, and
the salty sea spray, my flowers are stunted and my
vegetables are puny."

On the morning of the fifth day, Nathan and his
mother watched from the cottage stoop as the great
canoes, drawing deeply in the water with all the
wealth they were taking home, paddled out into the
bay. Gradually, the canoes grew smaller and smaller.
For a long time, when he could no longer make out
the canoes distinctly, Nathan could see the light
reflecting from the paddles all pulling in unison.

"Take a good look, son," his mother said, with deep
emotion. "One day you'll be able to say you saw those
beautiful canoes."

"You think they'll all be gone, Mother?"

"Everything will, Nathan. Everything passes, everything changes."

He was surprised by the sadness in her voice. His mother never gave in to melancholy.

As they watched, the last trace of the canoes vanished in the sparkling waters of the Strait.

Change was in the offing, as his mother seemed to have predicted. When the *Anna Rose* returned to Neah Bay a few days later, Nathan helped the Makahs paddle Captain Bim out to the steamer. Bim had sold the trading post and his cottage to mild-speaking Jack Kane, the man with the intense blue eyes.

As Captain Bim was paddled across Neah Bay toward the *Anna Rose,* which was anchored near Waadah Island, Bim wasn't looking ahead, toward the steamer. He was looking back, toward Neah Bay, at the canoes coming and going, and at the longhouses behind. "Twenty-two years," the trader mused.

"You'll miss it," Nathan said.

"Aye. Those little shacks people are building as they move out of the longhouses—none of those were here when I came."

"You'll have your ice-cream parlor?"

Captain Bim's foot struck his sea chest. Nathan could hear the rattle of coins inside. "He paid me half as much as was stolen from me. It's the best I could do, a better price than I would have guessed, and he paid cash. I can only hope it's enough."

"Lucky Mr. Kane had his money with him."

The broken bear of a man smiled his knowing smile and picked at the tangles of his beard. "Of course, Kane came to Neah Bay expressly to buy the business. I figured that out, boy. He must have heard about it in Port Townsend, obviously. He was a good card player, Kane was. Never acted very interested in Neah Bay."

"Is the trading post a good business?"

"Of course it is! There's no competition. I suppose I was a fool to sell it, but I'm ready to move on. These last weeks since I was robbed, my heart just wasn't in it."

"Do you still think Dolla Bill did it?"

"He loves money, that much is certain. As I warned Kane, for everything Bill does, he thinks he should be paid on the spot. He doesn't comprehend the idea of a salary."

"Why would Dolla Bill keep working in the store if he has a whole lot of money hidden somewhere?"

"I don't know, I don't know. I can't pretend to understand the workings of Dolla Bill's mind. Perhaps it was your phantom fugitive from the Cape who discovered my box. I can almost see him now, living in the finest rooms of the finest hotel on Nob Hill in San Francisco, enjoying the finest meals, the finest wines— at my expense."

Captain Bim forced himself to look away from Neah Bay. His eyes were misty, and slow to clear. When at last he spoke again, he looked straight at Nathan and clapped him on the shoulder. "Let this be said, before I go. You, Nathan MacAllister, are a persistent, nay, a *stalwart* young man. Had I listened to the better angels of my nature, we would have been great friends. I wish you the very best in life, as you surely deserve it."

Nathan had never seen a grown man other than his

father apologize over something of consequence. Instantly, he was overcome with his own regrets. "Good luck in Port Townsend, Captain Bim. I wish I'd been a better friend for you. Next time . . ."

"Ah yes. As some sage once said, Where there's life, there's hope."

·14·

Forty Tons of Fury

In six of their great canoes, the Makahs were hunting gray whales out beyond the curve of the earth.

Nathan was among them, paddling just forward of the stern in one of the eight-man canoes. His father had known the danger Nathan could only guess at, but he had also known how badly Nathan wanted to go. "I was your age when I went to sea," his father had allowed, and then Zachary MacAllister had given his consent.

It had begun when his father learned that the Makahs, in the old days, had used Tatoosh Island as their best whale-sighting post. After the lighthouse had been built on the island, they hadn't been allowed to use it anymore. So Captain MacAllister had invited them back to Tatoosh, and indeed, they'd sighted whales from the incomparable vantage point of the catwalk atop the lighthouse.

As he paddled, Nathan kept scanning the horizon for the spouts of the whales they were chasing. But he was momentarily looking over his shoulder at the mountainous profiles of Vancouver Island and snow-capped Mount Olympus rising above Washington Territory, when, simultaneously, wild yells went up from the six canoes.

Every crewman began to paddle in double-time. No more than a half mile away, the dark rounded shape of a whale's head broke the surface, and the whale spouted high into the air. In the bow, Lighthouse George had his keen eyes fastened on the whale. His harpoons were at the ready, their thick shafts resting between the ears of the carved wolf head at the prow of the canoe. The bottom of the canoe was filled with whaling gear, including the bulky inflated sealskin floats. Nathan paddled with all his might, and he felt the forward surge of the canoe as it sliced up and through the great gray rollers.

Nathan heard several more whale blows that he couldn't see. It's more than one whale, he realized. Then he saw a whale's flukes rise above the water. A rising tail meant the whale was diving.

The whales had sounded. With none in sight, the canoes raced to the north, at an angle intended to intercept the whales when they next appeared. It was an undeclared race, and a silent one, each canoe wishing to be the first to harpoon a whale.

When the canoes had gone as far as they intended to go, the Makahs quit paddling for a few minutes. The crewmen on all the canoes looked and listened intently for the blow of a whale. Lighthouse George selected a harpoon, with its sharpened mussel-shell point and antler-tip barbs. He checked the rope where it was attached to the harpoon head, checked the seal-skin floats fixed to the rope, checked the coil in the basket at his feet.

Now the canoes, each according to its leader's directions, paddled silently this way or that in hopes of being the closest to a whale when it broke the surface.

As it happened, a whale not only came to the surface, it breached, completely upright, not thirty yards from Lighthouse George's canoe, which was the closest. Half the whale's length rose above the water, and Nathan saw a fin flapping in the air like a stubby wing. Water streamed down the whale's barnacled sides in the moment before the immense gray fell back into the sea with a resounding crash.

All paddles, including Nathan's, were instantly back in the water, paddling full strength. With a powerful back-sweeping motion of the rudder paddle, the man behind him aimed the bow of the canoe directly at the whale. The rest of the canoes chased to catch up as fast as they could.

The whale, Nathan realized as they drew close, would have to spout and draw breath before it could sound. Their canoe was drawing closer and closer to the side of the whale. They were so close Nathan could see the gray's eye and the countless tiny barnacles attached to its skin.

It was at this moment, as Lighthouse George was poised to plant the harpoon, that Nathan heard a ripping, cutting sound, along with a *whoosh* of escaping air, coming from somewhere in the center of their canoe. Nathan looked and saw six inches of knife blade, like a thing alive, sticking out of the largest of the sealskin floats. The knife blade was ripping the bag apart from the inside. Abruptly, the terrified crewmen stopped paddling. From within the float, a hand, an arm, and then a shoulder appeared, followed by the shaven, pocked, tattooed, and weirdly grinning head of Dolla Bill.

Before the astounded crewmen could even react, the magician was out of the float, scrambling forward and reaching for one of the spare harpoons propped up in the bow of the canoe. Suddenly the canoe was drenched by the spume of the whale. Dolla Bill stood up alongside Lighthouse George. He fully meant to sink his own harpoon, but the moment had been lost and the whale was drawing away. The gray's back rounded high in the air and it sounded with a great slap, the tail's broad flukes striking barely forward of the canoe.

As the beaten waves washed over the canoe and sent it bobbing violently in the whale's wake, the crewmen fell on Dolla Bill, tore the harpoon from his hand, and dragged him to the bottom of the canoe. Dolla Bill put up no resistance. He looked surprised and hurt, like a child, as if he'd expected them to applaud his stunt. A knife was drawn. Dolla Bill would have been killed in the next instant if Lighthouse George had not raised his voice.

The rest of the canoes went racing after the whale.

On the bottom of the canoe, Dolla Bill suddenly began laughing, as if he had played the greatest joke imaginable. He was about to have his hands tied when, again, Lighthouse George forbade it. Dolla Bill calmed himself and sat cross-legged in the bottom of the canoe, still as a statue. The crewmen, Nathan included, took up their paddles and resumed the chase.

Nathan wondered if any of the canoes could catch up to the whale now. Lighthouse George exhorted his paddlers to pull, and pull harder. Nathan's lungs screamed for air. He thought his back would break. All the while, his mind raced. How could Dolla Bill have hidden inside the float? Had he sewn himself in? How had he managed to breathe? Why had he done it? Didn't he know that only a chief or the son of a chief could harpoon a whale? Dolla Bill was crazy!

By luck or by skill, one of the canoes was close to the whale when it next broke the surface. With a burst of speed the canoe closed as the whale blew a second time. Nathan saw the harpooner stand in the bow as the animal rounded its long streaming back out of the water. The gray was preparing to sound, but it was a moment too late. The brawny harpooner thrust the heavy harpoon into the whale's back behind its shoulder. Almost at once, the shaft snapped free, leaving the weapon's head embedded in the whale.

The crew of the canoe that harpooned the whale instantly began back-paddling from the whale as fast as they could. Nathan saw the long line whipping out of the bow of the canoe, and he saw several floats attached to the line fly out of the canoe as well. The man in the stern tossed a rope to the man in the bow of a second canoe that had caught up to them. In a moment, the second canoe was attached to the first, and a third was attached to the second.

Lighthouse George's canoe was closing fast on the third canoe—he yelled for his men to try harder to reach it. It was all happening so fast.

Maddened by the harpoon head and hindered by

the floats it was dragging, the whale raised its bulk out of the water and sounded.

The lead canoe, despite its effort to back away, was nearly swamped by the wave raised by the whale.

Nathan saw the harpoon rope go taut, and the three attached canoes shoot forward suddenly like arrows. Barely in time, Lighthouse George's quick hands caught a thrown rope from the third canoe, and he secured it in an instant. Nathan felt his canoe go shooting, leaping, fast, fast, powered now by forty tons of whale.

The sounding whale, in its effort to reach the bottom, made a commotion that stirred the sea as if a volcano were erupting underwater. With its sheer strength, the whale had pulled the floats underwater, and it seemed the lead canoe might be pulled under as well. The shape of the whaling canoe's high prow, its own size and bulk, and the skill of its paddlers barely combined to keep it afloat.

The canoes slowed, and Nathan wondered if the rope to the whale had broken. The answer came as the animal suddenly burst from the sea. The lines connecting the four canoes went tight as a bowstring, and the canoes once more shot forward at high speed in the wake of the whale. The fifth and sixth canoes, moments away from attaching to the rest, were quickly left behind.

There was no paddling to be done now. Clinging to thwarts and gunwales, George's crew kept their weight low in the canoe. Nathan had never imagined moving at such high speed. He was soaked to the skin by the spray flying off the canoe. The cold wind whipped his face and his hair as the canoes sped away from land toward the sun, low in the sky over the open ocean. Dolla Bill caught Nathan's eye and grinned, as if they were having a lark. Nathan ignored him.

Nathan realized that there was no chance that they would be able to get back to land before the sun set. It was the end of June—the days were long, and the twilight lingered, but even so, the light wasn't going to last nearly long enough.

If the Makahs were worried, they weren't showing it. They were singing.

It was miles and miles until the whale finally slowed. All three canoes behind the first one disengaged themselves from the train. They wanted to be free to attack the whale, Nathan realized.

Lighthouse George signaled his men to bring him alongside the whale. The whale was on Nathan's side of the canoe, fully as long as the canoe or longer, and nearly so close he could reach out and touch it. Standing in the bow, George thrust the tip of his harpoon deep into the whale's back. The thick braided rope, made of whale sinew and the inner bark of cedar, went flying off its coil, and so did three floats.

As fast as they were able, Nathan and the rest of the paddlers were trying to back the canoe away from the whale. Suddenly the whale's flukes seemed to fill the sky above them. Get away from the tail! Nathan thought as he back-paddled with all the strength he had in him. But the immense flukes swept the canoe in their downward motion, and the canoe was broken in two, like a toy, and tossed high in the air.

He found himself swimming for his life in the freezing Pacific. The front half of the canoe, along with the floats, was being dragged away behind the whale. Men were everywhere in the water. He realized he was going to be able to manage until one of the other canoes could pick him up; he was a strong swimmer. But where was Lighthouse George? Dolla Bill and the other men were swimming toward the nearest canoe, but George wasn't among them. *Where was George?*

Nathan looked behind him. A man was floating facedown in the water, knocked unconscious or dead. He swam to the man, before he might sink, and turned him over, kicking to buoy the man's face above the water. It was his friend.

Nathan called to the other canoes as he struggled with all his strength to keep George's face above the water. Don't be dead, my friend, he prayed, please don't be dead.

The two canoes that had disengaged from the whale had rescued the other swimmers and were paddling back toward Nathan. Lighthouse George was lifted unconscious into a canoe. Nathan was the last to be pulled in. He crawled to Lighthouse George on the bottom of the canoe, where several of George's men were wrapping him in a bearskin cape. Nathan determined that his friend was breathing. George's forehead was badly swollen where it might have been struck by the whale's flukes or by the canoe. Tears were streaming from Dolla Bill's eyes. "Poor George," he kept crying. "Poor George."

As soon as the paddles floating on the surface were retrieved, the two canoes resumed the chase. By the time they caught up and tied on, all three of the canoes ahead of them had harpoons in the whale. The whale had slowed considerably. It was dragging

118

twelve floats now and five canoes, and the wreckage of a sixth one.

The whale had strength yet. It sounded, but was soon back at the surface. It blew again, and tried to sound, and then towed them farther still to the west. Two more harpoons were added, and many more floats. The whale continued to beat the sea to froth with its struggles until its tail was all entangled with lines and floats. The Makahs waited patiently, knowing the whale was doomed now and would eventually exhaust itself.

Nathan wished it would end. The sun was setting, he couldn't see the land any longer, and the whale was turning the ocean red from a number of deep gashes. *Kwaddis*, the great gray whale, had very little strength left.

At last the hunters thrust long, thin-shafted killing lances into the whale, trying for the spot that would kill it. The whale cried and moaned with a humanlike voice, as a human mother might moan, Nathan thought, in agony over a dead child. Then a Makah stepped from a canoe to the whale's back and, with a deep-planted lance, found the place, which sent blood spouting high in the air from the whale's blowhole. With a last convulsion, the whale rolled on its side, dead.

The man who had dealt the death blow was now swimming alongside the canoe. He was handed a bone awl and a coil of light line made of braided cedar. With dusk gathering, he dove under the water, and stayed down for a long time, perhaps a minute, before he surfaced, recovered his strength, and dove again. Nathan finally saw what he was doing—sewing the whale's mouth shut so the whale wouldn't fill with water and sink.

The five canoes began to tow the whale back to Neah Bay. Before long it was pitch dark, and Nathan had no idea where land was. But the Makahs knew, from the currents and from the stars.

Fearing for George's life, Nathan paddled into the night. Paddling helped him keep from freezing. The crescent moon rose. He did his part to tow the immense dead weight of the whale toward the dim hulking shape of land. It became the longest night of his life. The sun was rising as the canoes neared the cliffs of Tatoosh and entered the Strait.

Lighthouse George was conscious now. Somebody helped him sit up. But something was wrong with him. George didn't recognize Nathan. Nathan didn't think he recognized anybody, and he couldn't move his left leg. He didn't seem to have any pain in the leg; it seemed he couldn't feel it at all.

Nathan could see his father on the catwalk of the lighthouse with a spyglass, and waved to him. His father waved back. His father wouldn't know anything was wrong.

The five canoes towed the whale into Neah Bay on the afternoon's high tide. Nathan had never felt so weary in his life. They were met at the beach by hundreds of villagers singing to welcome the whale. Lighthouse George, carried out of the canoe and laid flat on the bearskin cape on the beach, couldn't recognize Rebecca.

Young Carver was called, the man who made the canoes. He probed George's lifeless leg and looked into his eyes. Old Jefferson listened as George's crew pointed to Dolla Bill, who was walking away toward the trading post. With much acting out, they told how Dolla Bill had suddenly emerged from the float during the whale hunt, and how Lighthouse George had spared his life.

Jefferson glanced over to the trading post porch, where Dolla Bill had joined Jack Kane. Much excited, Dolla Bill seemed to be conveying his exploits to his new employer. Nathan wondered if Jefferson was going to pronounce judgment on Dolla Bill, but the old chief said nothing other than *"Skookum-man."* It seemed that since George had already spared his life, Dolla Bill wasn't going to have to answer to a lesser sentence.

Hundreds of people pulled on ropes and, bit by bit, worked the massive body of the whale up onto the beach. Its head was sprinkled with eagle down and it was honored with more singing and ceremony.

The harpooner who had struck first opened up the whale first. Soon men were pulling sections of blubber from the midsection of the whale. The blubber was heavy and slippery—it looked like the men were trying to pull five-hundred-pound blankets off a bed.

Lighthouse George could talk, but he still couldn't recognize Rebecca or anyone else. Young Carver had a number of men lift George into one of the small canoes and carry him up to bed in his longhouse.

·15·

The King and His Fool

Even though he was close to the carcass, Nathan watched the last of the butchering as if from a distance. He felt lost without Lighthouse George. He tried to help Rebecca carry away her share of the blubber and the gelatinous red flesh underneath, but she shooed him away. The quick laughter from all the other women working on the carcass made him feel foolish for inviting himself into the women's domain.

He went to George's bed behind the partition in his corner of the longhouse and found him lying on his back, with eyes open and staring aloft. George wasn't looking at the huge beams or the strips of fish and seal meat hanging from the rafters; he wasn't looking at anything. "How are you feeling, George?" Nathan asked.

His friend's dark eyes took Nathan in, but showed no recognition. Lighthouse George went back to staring into the rafters.

"It's me, Tenas Mac. It's *Yaw-ka-duke*, your partner."

When George didn't reply, Nathan sat with him without speaking, and finally he wandered back to the whale. Screaming seagulls by the hundreds and hundreds, along with the ravens, were cleaning up the dregs of the butchering and picking at the bones of the massive, reddish skeleton. The Makahs had taken all the bone they needed, as well as all the whale's sinew—and even its stomach, bladder, and intestines for use as bags to store food or oil.

Nathan checked in on his mother, and was surprised to find her in bed. "I've just taken cold," she said, "but I don't think I should teach any sewing for a few days. Tell them at the Agency. . . ."

"I will," he agreed.

He must have let his disappointment show, and even the fear that had quickly chilled his heart. "Don't worry," she assured him. "I'll be over this in a few days. I'm just so upset with myself. Here you've taken a swim in the Pacific Ocean, and you're evidently healthy as a horse."

"I am, Mother," he assured her.

"But promise me that was the last of your whale-hunting career."

"I can't believe how brave the Makahs are," he replied.

"You have as much courage as they do. And you love the wild, wide ocean, just like your father. But all the same, for my sake . . ."

"I'll promise, Mother, if you'll promise to get well once and for all."

"I will, Nathan, I will. They keep saying at the Agency that the doctor from Port Townsend is going to visit in Neah Bay to see patients. I've written; he's sending some medicine."

"I'm so afraid for Lighthouse George, and Rebecca."

"An injury to the head, like his, could take time."

"Will he get better?"

"He might, but he might not. All we can do is pray for him, I'm afraid."

"I'm going to the store to get you tea and sugar. I'll warm you some milk, too."

As Nathan approached the trading post, he found several Makah women with empty baskets waiting on the porch, confused about whether they should go in. He could hear the sound of laughter inside and what sounded like the whirring of thrown knives.

He was right about the knives. As he opened the screen door and stepped inside, he saw two enormous knives quivering in the wall down at the end of the long counter. Kane was pulling his from the bull's-eye he had chalked onto the wall, and Dolla Bill was cackling with glee. "Whale man!" Dolla Bill shouted as he spied Nathan. "What you like? Everything for sale!"

Nathan's eyes went from Dolla Bill to Kane. The Panama hat and the white suit and shoes were gone; Kane had found trousers, boots, and a coarse blue cotton shirt in the store. Nathan was struck by the man's physical presence. Though he wasn't especially tall, his shoulders were extraordinarily wide, and he was narrow at the hip.

"Come in, Nathan," Kane said with a friendly smile. The man strode the length of the counter with the confidence and grace of a lion. He hadn't shaved in several days, and his thick stubble was dark in contrast to his golden hair. The man's voice was mild and warm, as ever, his bright blue eyes full of care. "How's your mother? She's quite sick, you know. You should take care of her better."

"That's why I'm here," Nathan said. "To get some things for her. Tea and sugar."

"Good, good. I'm happy to hear it."

Down at the end of the counter, Dolla Bill pulled another knife from the display case and began to juggle the three of them. Nathan was awed by his dexterity: one slip and the results would be bloody. The bone handle of one of the knives, Nathan noticed, was decorated with an engraving of a ship, either a clipper ship or a steamer outfitted with sails, he couldn't tell which.

He remembered, vaguely, hearing something not so long ago about a knife with a clipper ship design on its grip. His thoughts jumped to his father's upcoming birthday. For a moment he thought of the knife as a possible gift, if the ship was indeed a clipper and not a steamer. But the knife would be expensive, and his father didn't like the kind of presents that cost money, anyway.

"There are some women out on the porch," Nathan said to the new trader, with one eye on the knives in motion. "I think they don't know if they should come in or not." He said it lightly, as if Kane hadn't noticed they were there. It seemed unlikely that Kane hadn't. Nathan was determined to make friends with the new trader and to avoid saying anything that might be taken amiss.

"Well, of course they should come in," Kane said with a warm smile, waving to the women. "We're in business, aren't we, Bill?"

"Business!" the outcast shouted.

The Makah women, watching the magician through the screen door, made no move to come inside. "I'm not sure they trust Dolla Bill," Nathan whispered.

"Did you see his trick on the Indians' little whaling expedition?" Kane asked.

"I was in the same canoe. He's lucky they didn't kill him."

"A tragic misunderstanding—he thought they would love him for it. They had admired his previous work, and this was his greatest trick."

Dolla Bill, while juggling the knives, had overheard. Tears were streaming from his eyes.

"His feelings were terribly hurt," Kane explained. "Like many great artists, Dolla Bill is a misunderstood soul."

Nathan wondered if Kane was joking. It didn't seem so. Why should he defend Dolla Bill? "Dolla Bill acts crazy," Nathan whispered across the counter.

With a smile, Kane said, "No more than the king's fool in Shakespeare's plays. Do you read Shakespeare?"

"My mother does."

"Then she would understand that the fool's nonsense is actually the truth. You see, Dolla Bill is not only a magician and a contortionist, but a philosopher as well."

"A philosopher?" Nathan repeated. Kane seemed

such a man of the world, so intelligent. Perhaps it took a genius to recognize a genius.

Three women came inside. From their baskets, they brought out eight *sla hal* sets among them—sixteen of the bones—and put them on the counter. Kane paid them with a twenty-dollar gold piece, and they left. Nathan was amazed at the price.

Dolla Bill picked up one of the unmarked *sla hal* pieces. He studied the cylinder for a few moments, then twisted it in opposite directions. It pulled apart. Dolla Bill looked disappointed, as if he'd been looking for something to fall out.

Nathan commented, "I didn't know they were hollow."

"Some of them are," Kane said. The new trader took the two sections of the bone piece from Dolla Bill and fitted them back together with a twist. "Look how cleverly they're made, Nathan. You can barely see the joints even if you're looking for them."

"A dollar-and-some for one of those seems like a lot of money," Nathan said.

"Not really," Kane replied confidently, and he opened a cabinet that was behind the counter. Nathan saw dozens of *sla hal* pieces inside.

"Do you think they're valuable?" Nathan asked. He was already thinking where he could acquire two, and make a little money, but he instantly rejected the idea of robbing a grave. "Captain Bim paid for bricks from the bakery of the old Spanish fort."

Kane laughed contemptuously. "Who cares about bricks? These bone game pieces are unique works of art! I think collectors will be very interested in them. Do you know of any more?"

Nathan hesitated, just a second. "No," he answered.

Dolla Bill sprang forward with a devilish smile. "Tenas Mac not tell the truth."

"Not any that are mine," Nathan added quickly, surprised that Dolla Bill had read him so easily. And then he explained, "Lighthouse George has a pair."

Dolla Bill brought his pocked, scarred face inches from Nathan's face, and stared. "Still not tell the truth!" he sang, and then he danced away.

Kane was scrutinizing Nathan with his piercing blue eyes. Suddenly he quit. "For you, three dollars a pair," Kane said with a smile. "That's good money. See if you can find us some. How much did Bim pay for a brick?"

"Two bits."

Nathan considered the idea of the bone pieces as art. Surely they were ingenious, and they had a certain beauty, but Kane hadn't been around long enough to see all the other things the Makahs made that were even more artistic.

"What about carved cedar boxes?" he suggested. "Those are works of art. The wood is perforated where the joints are going to be, but not all the way through. When they steam the cedar and bend it, there's not even a joint. That's why they're waterproof. Collectors should like that, and especially with all the designs that are carved on the outside. What about masks? The Makahs have masks all over the place. And they could make more. . . ."

Kane held up his hand. "Right now I'll just start with the *sla hal* pieces. It's the bone game that's caught my fancy. Those other things . . . yes, they're beautiful, and maybe people will want them. One step at a time. If the bone game pieces sell as well as I think they will, in cities like New York and London and Paris, then we'll have prepared the market for the rest, which will be much more difficult and expensive to ship."

"What about the canoes?" Nathan said, wondering aloud. "The canoes are the most beautiful works of art of all."

"I like you," Kane said. "You don't think small. Maybe we can sell some of the canoes to museums."

"Oh, I don't want to sell them."

"Why not?"

"I don't know. I was just trying to figure out your business, I guess."

"Well, there's got to be more to it than selling tea and sugar. Bill, let's take care of our customer." The new trader laughed, as if he'd said something funny, then added, "Another day, another dollar."

Nathan went back home with a sense of unease. It was difficult to comprehend Kane. He was so dazzling, so self-assured, so knowledgeable, yet it didn't seem he'd chosen the sort of business that would suit him.

He remembered Dolla Bill taking one of the *sla hal* pieces apart as soon as the women brought them in. Dolla Bill had been looking for something inside.

Had he really been looking for something, or merely entertaining himself?

In the evening, Nathan told his mother all about Kane's idea of selling the bone game pieces as art.

She listened carefully, and then she said, "People in New York and London and Paris are known for driving up the prices of the latest thing that's fashionable. I suppose that artifacts from the Indians of the last remote tip of America might strike their fancy. Conceivably, they might even start playing the bone game as a new form of gambling."

"Maybe so," Nathan agreed. "Kane is a smart man. He must know something."

"Smart, but not kind," his mother said pointedly. She coughed a bit, then reached for her tea. "Kane has raised the prices on everything, even food. I don't understand it. The agent sees no fault in it; they've become fast friends."

After his mother had gone to bed, Nathan sat up trying to make sense of it all. He kept thinking about everything he had seen and heard in the store that day. Suddenly he remembered who had spoken of an engraving of a ship—a clipper ship—on the bone handle of a knife. Captain Bim had! Such a knife was one of the items stolen from the trading post several months before!

Instantly, Nathan's mind was racing. Was it a clipper ship on the grip of the knife Dolla Bill had been juggling in the store? If it was a clipper ship, then it must be Dolla Bill who'd robbed the trading post! No one had suspected him because he'd arrived weeks after the robbery, on the *Anna Rose*. But what if he'd been in Neah Bay earlier, in hiding? What if he'd been the one who made the footprints? What if he'd been aboard the *Burnaby*?

It was easy enough to imagine Dolla Bill, so skillful with knives, putting one in Captain Flagg's heart.

But why?

In the morning Nathan had a perfect reason for going back to the trading post. His mother was going to bake, and she needed flour and more sugar.

Dolla Bill was by himself. The Makahs seemed to be staying away. The magician was standing on a foot-ladder and suspending a wicker cage from a hook in the ceiling. Two large white chickens were clucking anxiously inside, as if they were concerned by seeing Dolla Bill's face close up.

"Hello, Tenas Mac," Dolla Bill called cheerfully as Nathan came through the door. "You like my parrots?"

"Yes indeed," Nathan said, eyeing the chickens. "Have you taught them to talk?"

With a grin, Dolla Bill said, "Teach them to die, maybe."

"It's not that much of a trick to make chicken soup."

Dolla Bill's hollow eyes went wide. "You like to see a new trick?"

Nathan shrugged. He wasn't sure he did.

Dolla Bill removed one of the chickens from the cage and shut the door on the other. Then he placed the chicken on the counter. It clucked nervously, walking to and fro, keeping one eye or the other on Dolla Bill, who had turned his head sideways, the way a chicken would do, and was staring with one eye and then the other at the chicken.

After a minute of this, the chicken dropped dead on the counter.

Nathan was stunned. "How did you do that?"

Dolla Bill was wide-eyed. "Not a trick!" he exclaimed.

"You said it was new. Where did you learn it?"

Dolla Bill laughed. "From Kane!"

Nathan was thinking as fast as he could. "Was Kane in the circus, too? Did you know him from before?"

"Met him here!" Dolla Bill cackled.

"One of those knives you were juggling yesterday . . . ," Nathan said evenly. "It had some kind of ship engraved on the handle."

Nathan was watching Dolla Bill's hollow eyes for the slightest reaction.

"Clipper ship," Dolla Bill said, with no hesitation at all.

Nathan was surprised by Bill's complete lack of wariness, but he didn't pause to think what it meant. He was prepared to ask certain questions, and he felt confident he could ask them without arousing suspicion. As long as everything he was about to say was the truth, Dolla Bill wouldn't get suspicious. "I was hoping it was a clipper ship, and not a steamer," Nathan explained. "My father used to be the captain of a Yankee clipper, and I was thinking what a wonderful birthday present it would make for him. How much does it cost?"

The clerk wagged his tatooed head. "Not for sale."

Nathan looked disappointed. "No? But why not?"

"Kane's own knife."

Nathan was surprised, deeply surprised. No wonder Dolla Bill hadn't been wary about the knife. Dolla Bill didn't even know one had been stolen from the store!

He tried his best not to let his surprise show. He knew instantly what this revelation meant, but he told himself not to think about Kane, not until later. "Well, could I at least take a look at it? I'd sure like to see it. Maybe I could talk Kane into selling it to me."

"It's not here," Dolla Bill said with a shrug. "Keeps it at his house. I'll ask him for you."

Suddenly Nathan realized he'd gone too far. He'd

thought he was being so careful, but he hadn't seen this coming. He'd made a serious mistake, an enormous mistake. "Oh, don't bother," he told Dolla Bill as lightly as he could. "On second thought, it's not such a good idea for a birthday present, since my father would never use it anyway. A clipper ship inside a bottle, or something like that, would be a better idea."

Nathan made his purchases without acting hasty. He kept hoping that Kane wouldn't walk in, but then he did. Kane was right there in the doorway, looking from him to Dolla Bill and back. It was hard for Nathan to look Kane straight in the face and act normal. The man was so powerful. The features of his face were hard as flint. Nathan could see that now.

Kane took another look at Nathan. "Close the store," he ordered Dolla Bill. "Let's go fishing."

Nathan held his breath, hoping Dolla Bill wouldn't mention the knife to Kane. In the several minutes it took for Dolla Bill to make change and for Nathan to leave the store, he didn't.

From a distance, Nathan watched as the two of them launched one of the fishing canoes and paddled into the bay toward Koitlah Point. How long could he hold his breath, hoping Dolla Bill wouldn't tell?

·16·
He Is with the Whale

Lighthouse George was walking again. Nathan sat with him down by the bay.

Nathan's mother had told him to keep talking to Lighthouse George, even if George wasn't talking back. "He might be hearing voices from a great distance," she'd said. "It's as if he's sitting on the bottom of the ocean—that's how I picture it. If you keep talking, he might recognize the sound of your voice, and find his way back up to the surface."

On one of Nathan's visits to the longhouse, he'd heard Young Carver give Rebecca a different explanation: "He is with the whale."

"Is that where you are?" Nathan asked Lighthouse George, whose gaze was fixed on the sea. "Are you with the whale?"

His fishing partner did not reply. He seemed so content looking out at that carpet of blue-green water sparkling with white.

Nathan was anything but content. Like twin chemicals concocting poison, dread and terror were welling up inside him, and he was feeling sicker by the moment.

"I remember how you said there's a little bit of good inside Dolla Bill," Nathan said to George. "I don't think that's true about Kane. It was him. I'd bet anything. He's been here all along. It was Kane in the cave! He must be laughing at me! He paddled away, but not when we thought, not when he took the canoe from Dolla Bill. He didn't leave until after his second robbery, when he stole Bim's money. Bim was right that someone was spying on him."

George sat, impassive. Nathan imagined that his words made as little sense to George now as the language of the Makahs made to Nathan. Still, he wanted to finish. Talking was helping him to think.

"Kane must have escaped with Bim's money in that second canoe, the one that disappeared from the village. He probably canoed along the coast all the way to Port Townsend. Then he came back all cleaned up on the *Anna Rose,* pretending to be a gentleman, and bought the trading post with Bim's own money!"

"Klo-she," Lighthouse George said placidly, his eyes still fixed on the sea.

"I know," Nathan responded. "It's good. The sea is good. I wish you could tell me what it means that Kane and Dolla Bill have gone somewhere now in one of the canoes. They left a couple of hours ago. They were looking for *sla hal* pieces before; what are they after now? Kane's after something—that's why he never left after he murdered the captain of the *Burnaby*! That's why he bought the trading post. He's a murderer, George. What's going to happen to me if Kane finds out I know about that knife?"

Nathan's thoughts were leading in more and more fearful directions. He knew he had to make himself think about something else. "Let's go see how Young Carver is coming along," he said, and stood up. Lighthouse George stood up as well and followed him to the village creek, where the whaling canoe was nearing completion.

George enjoyed watching Young Carver work. *"Klo-she,"* he said to Nathan.

"Do you remember Young Carver visiting you in the longhouse, and dancing and singing over you?"

George tilted his face up to the sun, and said, *"Klo-she."*

Young Carver was working in a sitting position inside the canoe. With a hand adze, chip by chip, he was thinning the sides of the hull. Think about how the canoe is made, Nathan told himself. Think about only that.

He remembered how, in the weeks before George had been hurt, he had figured out the canoe maker's method of achieving a perfectly uniform thickness. Young Carver had drilled dozens of small holes all the way through the hull. Then, from the outside, he'd tapped cedar pegs, all the same length, into the holes. Returning to the inside of the canoe, the holes were his guide as he chipped away wood. When he met the end of a peg, he knew to chip no farther, and he split out the wood between one peg and the next. That's what Young Carver was doing now, stripping lengths of wood between his markers.

Young Carver never spoke to anyone when he was working on the canoe, so Nathan wasn't surprised that the elder with the wispy gray beard didn't acknowledge George and him sitting only a few yards away. The canoe maker was one of the few Makahs who spoke some English, but he rarely used the white man's language. Young Carver had spoken for the first time in English to Nathan in the longhouse, when Nathan had been sitting day after day with George.

Nathan made himself think about the world of his family, uncontaminated by Kane and fears of Kane. Would the doctor come soon and help his mother get better? Could his mother get well enough for them to return to Tatoosh? Wouldn't the storms on Tatoosh only make her worse and worse? How long could his father live apart from his family?

Just then Nathan realized that Young Carver had paused at his work and was looking at him. Not at Lighthouse George, who was seated next to him, but at him. "Welcome early tomorrow," he said in English.

"Good," Nathan said, though he was confused. "Thank you."

"Bring canoe paddles, and bring him, too," Young Carver said, with a nod of his head toward Lighthouse George. "Sometime something make him remember."

Late in the afternoon Nathan walked Lighthouse George home to his longhouse. As they parted, Lighthouse George studied Nathan's face, trying hard to remember. "It's *Yaw-ka-duke*," Nathan reminded him. "Tenas Mac."

"Tenas Mac," Lighthouse George said, trying hard. But he couldn't remember.

Nathan went straight to his mother's cottage, without a glimpse of Kane or Dolla Bill. Inside, he felt safe. He wished he could tell her everything, but he thought he shouldn't. Her health was much too fragile. He should save it for his father.

No sleep. It wasn't possible.

In the morning, without a glimpse of Kane or Dolla Bill around the trading post, he went to George's long-house and brought him to the place up from the beach and beside the creek where Young Carver was making the whaling canoe. Fifteen men were helping today. This was highly unusual. Nathan set aside the two canoe paddles he had brought from the long-house. He didn't know what they might be for. He was happy to be among so many Makahs. He felt safe, for the time being.

Some of the men were carrying water from the creek, a canoe bailer full of water in each hand, and pouring it into the canoe. Young Carver and some others were selecting stones from the creek bed and placing them in four small fires that had been built not far from the canoe.

Nathan helped to carry water to the canoe while Lighthouse George watched the men bring rocks to the fires. When the bottom of the canoe had a foot of water in it, Young Carver signaled that it was enough. Men started bringing the superheated rocks to the canoe, on poles forked at one end, and dropping them into the canoe. Nathan helped with the stones. Every time one was dropped into the canoe, the water hissed and gave off a burst of steam. The rocks glowed red for a second or two, and then the cold water quenched their fire.

For several hours, red-hot stones were brought from the fires, and cold ones were retrieved from the canoe and returned to the fire. Finally the water in the canoe reached the boiling point, and clouds of steam rose all along the length of the canoe. A young boy was sent to get more help. Suddenly everyone who'd brought a canoe paddle picked it up and took it to the canoe. Nathan grabbed the two they had brought and gave one to Lighthouse George, who was just as confused as Nathan. In imitation of the other men, they stood at the side of the canoe and splashed the boiling water up against the insides of the canoe's hull.

Billowing clouds of steam engulfed them, and so did the pungent scent of wet cedar. The new men who had come to help kept bringing the fiery stones and retrieving the cold ones. The boiling and the splashing and the steaming continued for several hours. George had a contented expression on his face. He was speaking to Young Carver in Makah.

"Does he know you?" Nathan asked hopefully.

"No," the canoe maker replied. "He said he has to go to Tatoosh, but he can't remember why."

"To deliver the mail," Nathan suggested. "That must be what he's trying to remember."

"Tomorrow," Young Carver said, "we take the mail to Tatoosh, you and him and me."

Tomorrow, Nathan thought, tomorrow I'll see my father.

The sides of the canoe were softening and spreading outward in front of Nathan's eyes. Now he understood how the canoe achieved its graceful shape from a simple cedar log. He kept slopping the boiling water. Young Carver kept calling for hot rocks until he was satisfied that the flaring sides of the canoe had spread far enough. Then he and some assistants drove posts paired across from each other all along the length of the canoe to keep the upper edges from spreading any farther.

Finally Young Carver put in the thwarts and fastened them to the hull. The thwarts fixed the exact finished width of the canoe, and they would also serve as the paddlers' seats.

It was late in the day. Nathan stood back and admired the lines of the canoe. Exactly like the lines of a clipper ship's hull, he thought.

Nathan passed close by the trading post on the way home. Kane and Dolla Bill were walking up from the beach. They saw all the Makahs who were waiting for them to open the store. Kane just kept walking, toward his cottage. Dolla Bill, who'd lived inside the store since Kane's first day, shooed them all off the porch angrily in Chinook. *"Chako mahkook house tomolla!"*—"Come to the trading post tomorrow!"

"Tomolla!" he yelled after them.

Dolla Bill signaled for Nathan to come close. Nathan pretended at first he hadn't seen, but Dolla Bill persisted. Whatever it was, Nathan didn't want to hear it.

"Kane said to tell you that he's sorry he can't sell you his knife. He lost it today, over the water. Deep, deep water. He was killing a fish."

·17·
A Voice from Beyond the Grave

Young Carver didn't want to wait in the quarters attached to the base of the lighthouse while Nathan was visiting with his father. "We go up," he said to Nathan's father. "See if George can see whales."

"Good," Zachary MacAllister said. "Thank you for bringing the mail, and George, and my son." The two Makahs disappeared up the tower's winding stairs.

"Now tell me all about the whale hunt," Nathan's father said. "And how George was hurt."

"I will, later. Where are your assistants?"

"Scattered, to read their mail."

"They might walk in. Let's go to your office, where no one can hear us."

His father could see it was important. They went outside and down the path to the tiny building his father kept as his office, and his father closed the door behind them. "What, then? Is it your mother?"

"No, although she's not doing any better. It's about the man who bought the trading post."

His father had taken a seat, and offered Nathan the other. Nathan sat down, collected his thoughts, then told everything he suspected about Kane. His father listened carefully, and his face showed both surprise and grave concern. As Nathan finished his story, he told his father, "I still wonder what Kane and Dolla Bill are looking for, and whether they found it when they went off in the canoe."

His father stood, and looked out the windows to the sea for a long time. "What is it?" Nathan asked.

Zachary MacAllister turned back to Nathan. His gray eyes were deeply troubled. "You know far more than I could have ever guessed. Much too much."

Nathan was confused. "Do you know something I don't know?"

"I know the answers to both of your questions."

"You do?"

"Your second question first," his father said reluctantly. "As to whether they've found what they were looking for . . . yesterday the two of them paddled to Fuca's Pillar. We saw them land on it. They pulled the canoe onto a rock shelf at the base of the pillar. We were watching all of this with spyglasses, my assistants and I."

"When Alexander Flagg's brother came, he searched the pillar."

"Yes, but Kane climbed to the very top of it."

"The top! Is that possible?"

"I wouldn't have thought so, but I witnessed it with

my own eyes. He came back down safely as well—all without a rope, mind you. It was an amazing feat. In regards to what you suspect about the identity of the 'Hairy Man,' I could add that Kane took off his shirt before he climbed. That man's body is nearly as hairy as that of a beast."

"Do you think they found what they were looking for?"

"His behavior on Tatoosh afterward would indicate they did not."

"You mean they were here?"

"We had a strange meal together. Kane was as civilized as you might imagine, and Dolla Bill . . . well, his table manners left something to be desired. He made quite an impression on my assistants."

"Did Kane have an explanation for climbing Fuca's Pillar?"

"One of my assistants asked him that question. Kane said, 'For the sport of it.' He claims to have climbed the highest peak in the Andes of South America. Kane mentioned that he found something on top of Fuca's Pillar, although—"

"Some bones . . . a skeleton?" Nathan interrupted, to his father's amazement, and then he explained that Lighthouse George had told him of a young Makah stranded there. "Now tell me why Kane and Dolla Bill were on Tatoosh."

"They wouldn't say, of course, but they spent the afternoon scouring every inch of it they could reach, looking for something."

"So they didn't find it. . . . Did you say you could explain what it is they were after? How could you know?"

The retired sea captain bit his lip. "From a letter," he answered reluctantly. "A letter I received some weeks ago. You'll have to forgive me for not showing it to you then. I thought your welfare and your mother's would best be served by keeping it from you. Especially you, with your curiosity and your determination. I knew its contents would put you in harm's way. I hadn't accounted for how much you could surmise on your own. Knowing as much as you do, you'd best know the rest."

With that, his father brought out a bundle of letters from the bottom drawer of his desk, and withdrew one from the middle of the stack. "This is a copy that was made for me of a letter written by the murdered captain of the *Burnaby* to his brother, Jeremiah, shortly before his death. His brother sent it to me after he returned to Portland from his visit in Neah Bay. I didn't receive it until around the time of the big potlatch. In a note attached to the letter, Jeremiah Flagg said that he had learned of me from the captain of the boat he had chartered in Port Townsend. He regretted having no further time to try to resolve the circumstances of his brother's death, though he doubted that his brother's murderer could have escaped the wreck and swum to shore."

"Dolla Bill said that the 'hairy white *skookum-man*' who took his canoe 'swam like a fish'!"

"He must have been able to swim like a fish—you know what it's like around the Chibahdehl Rocks. Jeremiah Flagg went on to say in his note that in the event that the man survived, as the Makahs' early report of footsteps on the beach in the vicinity of the Cape might have suggested, he wanted me to know something about the man, as much as the letter he was sending conveyed. He thought that, being a retired ship's captain, I would especially want to see justice done."

Nathan's father unfolded the letter and handed it to him. "Now, read."

Dear Jeremiah,

I regret that it has been so many years since I have written. I trust that you are thriving in Portland and that your address remains the same. I hope in the coming year to visit in Portland, as I am no longer sailing to the Sandwich Islands. I am now engaged in the transport of lumber from the thriving young towns of Puget Sound, in Washington Territory, to San Francisco.

At the moment I am on my second voyage north, direct from San Francisco to Port Townsend, on the Burnaby. *The* Burnaby *will be docked at Port Townsend once we reach Puget Sound, for most of a week. During that time I intend to do some sightseeing of a highly unusual nature, which is the subject of my letter to you. I will be visiting the very tip of Washington Territory, in the vicinity of Cape Flattery, on a treasure-hunting expedition.*

"Treasure!" Nathan exclaimed, looking up from the letter. "Of course! Captain Bim told me a legend of a Spanish treasure, but I never took it seriously enough! I never thought it had anything to do with all this!"

"It's a Spanish treasure Kane's after, for certain," his father agreed. "Now read on."

Permit me, Jeremiah, to begin at the beginning, three years previous. A dying priest aboard my ship at that time, a Spaniard, entrusted me—burdened me, as I've come to realize—with a tale passed down to him as an inheritance. The tale concerned his grandfather, the Spanish commander of a fort in the Strait of Juan de Fuca in the last decade of the previous century. According to the priest, his grandfather was in possession of a fortune in bullion when he was forced to abandon the fort in Neah Bay. Fearing he was about to be intercepted by the English, the Spaniard left the treasure behind. Realizing that he might be killed or captured by the English, he made an ingenious map in two parts, neither of which would function without the other.

The maps were hidden inside two small bone pieces carved by the local Indians. One of these pieces, according to the priest, the commander hid in the wild environs of Neah Bay, in a location he described to me rather exactly before he died.

The commander kept the other map. As we know, the English succeeded in chasing the Spanish from the Northwest. The commander eluded capture by the English but died in Spain before he could attempt a return, to enemy territory, to recover the fortune. The bone piece with his map is now in my possession, having been given me by the priest.

I hesitate to describe the exact location where the priest told me that the corresponding piece is hidden. As you well know, the privacy of the mails cannot be trusted. More so, I fear those details being discovered by a partner I have engaged in this enterprise, who is presently aboard the Burnaby *and whom I have come to distrust.*

Regrettably, I did not distrust this partner at the time I shared the priest's secret with him. His name is Simon Peterson, or so he says—I have come to doubt his truthfulness almost completely.

I met this Peterson on the Barbary Coast, which, as you likely know, is a district along the docks in the port of San Francisco. It is a colorful place in the extreme, a crossroads of seafaring men the world over. It was there I befriended a man of unique talents, this Simon Peterson, an educated man, an adventurer, and a man of immense personal charm. The tales he related at the docks would seem beyond belief, if he weren't so mild, convincing, and engaging in his manner of telling them.

Peterson's physical prowess lends plausibility to the adventures he recounted from the remote jungles of the Amazon, where he claimed to have lived with headhunters, to the savannas of Africa, where he claimed to have wrestled with a lion and put a knife into its heart. He appears something of a lion himself: blond-haired, long-maned, with an immense beard.

The first time I laid eyes on him, he had just accepted a bet, the bets of many men, that he could swim through the cold, seething waters of San Francisco Bay to Alcatraz Island. No one thought it possible, as drownings are a virtual certainty in those waters if a sailor so much as falls from a ship.

This Peterson stripped to the waist, kicked off

his shoes, and dove into the bay. As you have already guessed, he survived his perilous swim and collected all bets. I was taken by Peterson's triumph and by his mild manner upon being accorded the cheers and congratulations of hundreds at the dock. Thereafter I found his tales from the four corners of the earth entirely believable. Many of these tales were conveyed solely to me; we had become fast friends. Peterson's preoccupation was treasure. He spoke of his searches in the West Indies for sunken galleons laden with gold, and of fabulous treasures that others had already found there.

At that time, I must say, I did not myself actually believe the account the priest had told me. It was merely a wonderful story and one which I felt compelled to share with my new friend. It was his belief in the priest's story that began to convince me that it might have some truth behind it, and might indeed, as Peterson believed, lead us directly to a fortune in gold.

We declared ourselves partners. I showed him the bone piece I carry on my person; I showed him the map inside. I told him that the second map, according to the priest, was hid "in the wild environs of Neah Bay, in a place the local Indians would not go." As I was about to tell him the exact nature and location of the place, I held myself back, feeling a twinge of fear, though at the time I had no reason to doubt his faithfulness. When Peterson pressed me, I explained, only half in jest, that if he knew everything, he would have no use for me. "Of course," he agreed good-naturedly.

The day before we sailed, I happened to be walk-

ing the streets of Chinatown. A crowd was watching a performer. From its fringes I discovered that the performer was none other than Peterson. The entertainment: killing a live chicken by staring at it. I swear he did this. As you may well imagine, he collected bets from all around.

I withdrew before he noticed me, though I cannot be sure of it. The man's powers of concentration while appearing to be looking elsewhere are nothing less than extreme. At any rate, I began to wonder if I had compromised my safety by entering into a partnership with a man of dubious if not sinister character, with nothing less than a fortune in bullion at stake to bring out the worst in his nature.

As inconsequential as the scene in the street may sound, it began to engender a fear in my own heart that has grown by the hour from that moment. Despite my best efforts at disguising my sudden and utter lack of confidence in him, Peterson sensed my anxiety with uncanny quickness.

Try as I might, I couldn't think of a reason I might put forward for disincluding him in the voyage. Not one that Peterson would believe. On the morning we were to sail, he was late. I gave orders to prevent him from boarding if he arrived at the last moment. To my immense relief, we sailed without him, or so I believed. He appeared when we were several hours out of port, explaining that he had slept aboard the ship.

It is my intention to have no more to do with Peterson after we reach Port Townsend. It would be folly to allow him to accompany me to Neah Bay.

GHOST CANOE

*If we were to discover a treasure, I have little doubt
I would be dead moments later. When I see Peterson about the ship, I have the sense that he knows
exactly what I am thinking; namely, that I am
planning on parting ways with him when we dock.*

*I have begun to carry a pistol on my person. I
believe that he has learned of my orders that would
have banned him from boarding. I have deduced
that Peterson is considering murdering me at sea.
If I will not provide him with the details I withheld
from him, what does he need me for? If he were to
murder me for the map I am carrying, he might
well be able to find the location of the second map
by proceeding to the Indian village at Neah Bay,
ascertaining locations that tradition forbids the
Indians from visiting, and searching them. I was
a fool to have ever told him so much!*

*It is possible, Jeremiah, that I am mistaken about
Peterson, in which case I will write again from
Port Townsend to reassure you.*

*If I come to harm, it is my hope that you will be
able to have this man brought to justice.*

With great trepidation, your brother Alexander

Nathan gave the letter back to his father. "Kane
really did murder Captain Flagg and throw him
overboard!"

"It would certainly seem so. Captain Flagg's suspi-
cions seem to have been well-founded."

"With the storm and then the fog, the crew couldn't
make it around Tatoosh and into the Strait without
their captain."

"It would appear not."

"Kane probably has Captain Flagg's *sla hal* piece. And he's looking for the other one," Nathan said. "He's been paying the Makahs to bring in every piece they can put their hands on."

"Now we know why. And we know that if Fuca's Pillar is indeed 'the place the Indians wouldn't go,' as it would seem to be from George's legend, then it appears that the Spanish priest's treasure has no basis in fact. Kane would have found it by now. Unless there's another place . . ."

Nathan's mind was racing. "A place the Indians wouldn't go . . . in the wild environs of Neah Bay . . ." In an instant of revelation, the ghost canoe came to mind, and the bone game pieces in the small cedar box. It would have made perfect sense for the Spaniard to hide the second map in an old Makah burial!

"What is it?" his father asked.

Nathan realized that if he told his father, his father might try to prevent Kane from finding the treasure before Kane could slip away. His father might not wait for the territorial marshal. For most of his life, he'd been the law aboard his ship. Even though his father knew how dangerous a man Kane was, he would act out of loyalty to a fellow ship's captain, even a dead one.

"I was wondering . . . ," Nathan replied, "does the territorial marshal have this letter?"

"He has the original. He says, to remove Kane from Neah Bay now would be to set him free, since no evidence, despite the strength of this letter, links him sufficiently to the death of Captain Flagg, the loss of the *Burnaby* and its men—or the theft of Captain

Bim's life savings, once the marshal becomes aware of that additional crime. The marshal intends to wait."

"Who knows in Neah Bay? The Indian agent?"

"No one. The knowledge would only endanger their lives. You're the one most at risk, Nathan. You know everything now. Remember what Captain Flagg said in his letter. Kane can read people, sense their fear."

"I won't let on, not in the least."

His father looked hard at him. "I'm counting on it. Remember, this man has already killed for this treasure, whether it be real or not. He'll kill again without the slightest hesitation."

"He already knows that I know about the knife that connects him to the burglary. . . . Would he kill me for that?"

"That would compromise his foothold at Neah Bay while he's searching for the treasure. He must assume that others, including your mother and me, know about the knife as well. With the knife now beyond recovery in the sea, you are merely an annoyance to be watched closely."

"Thank goodness!"

"Your knowledge of this letter, however, is another matter. Don't give him the slightest indication of what you know, or further provocation of any sort, Nathan. It would mean your life."

"I know."

His father waved from the top of the cliff as Nathan got into the canoe with Lighthouse George and Young Carver. Lighthouse George handed him a paddle and said, "Are the salmon running yet?"

"Not yet," Nathan replied, still preoccupied with the

conversation he had been having with his father. "But it's July now, and people say the salmon will run anytime."

"*Klo-she,*" George said.

It was then that Nathan noticed George's eyes. They seemed to have returned to the present moment. Was it possible?

"Do you remember me?" Nathan asked.

Lighthouse George smiled. "Sure, Tenas Mac. You're a good puller with the paddle. We catch lotsa fish, you and me."

Nathan looked to Young Carver, who said only, "Up in the lighthouse, he saw the whales."

George said, "Young Carver told me what happened on the whale hunt—what you did. I thank you."

"You would have been the first to harpoon the whale, George. If it weren't for Dolla Bill."

The Makah shook his head. "Trouble is George, not Dolla Bill. The whale remembers. Won't come back to your house if you dishonored him."

"We can always go fishing!"

"Salmon, Tenas Mac. Let's catch us some salmon."

·18·

No Pay, No Say

Lighthouse George wasted no time returning to his beloved country, the sea. "S'pose go fishing?" George said with a smile when Nathan answered the soft, familiar knock at the cottage door early the next morning. "I think Swimmer is back. I saw him in my dream."

They paddled around Koitlah Point toward the Chibahdehl Rocks, to find out if George was right about the salmon entering the Strait. In the shallow waters between the rocks and shore, George's keen eyes studied the waving kelp below the canoe until finally he said, *"Tyee."* Nathan squinted. At last he saw the flash of the large sleek fish weaving through the kelp, and understood why George had called them "chief." These were the biggest of all the salmon, the kings.

"How will you ever be able to use your fish harpoon?" Nathan wondered. "They're all spread out."

In reply, Lighthouse George took out his knife and smiled.

With a series of dives, while Nathan handled the canoe above, George opened a lane through the kelp bed. Then they anchored the canoe with heavy stones across the end of the lane. Within minutes, the king salmon were using the path, the easiest way through the kelp, and passing directly under their canoe. George brought up a thirty- or forty-pound king with his first try, and clubbed it smartly with his fish club. "This one special," he said, and marked it by passing a short piece of line through its mouth and gills.

Soon it was Nathan's turn to wield the harpoon and then haul the heavy kings over the side of the canoe.

As they were touching the beach at Neah Bay, with the canoe full of salmon, George held up that first salmon he had caught. It didn't take long for hundreds of people to appear on the beach. The first salmon signaled a welcome ceremony and festivities. There would be singing and dancing that night, and a feast of roasted salmon, George explained.

Rebecca was there on the beach, excited as everyone about the salmon. She waited patiently until the commotion died down, and then drew George away and spoke to him softly in Makah. She was obviously troubled about something she thought only George should hear. Nathan thought at first it might be his mother that Rebecca was talking about, but when he followed George to the gate of the village graveyard, he found out it was Kane. Kane was on his hands and knees, in broad daylight, pulling objects out of one of the little spirit houses built over the graves.

Nathan saw that Kane had pulled out plates, tea-cups, saucers, and a toy rocking chair. He was reaching inside the miniature door for something else. What in the world was he doing? Nathan looked quickly to Lighthouse George. The Makah was outraged.

George waved with his arm and called, "Get away, you! *Pelton tillicum!*"

Nathan guessed that Kane didn't know enough Chinook to realize that Lighthouse George had just called him a crazy person. But Kane knew well enough that he'd been chastised in no uncertain terms. "I'm putting everything back," he called to George.

George waited for Kane at the gate of the little cemetery. As the new trader approached, he said innocently, "Did I do something wrong? I was just so interested in the charming little houses. I didn't take anything. I wasn't sneaking around at night, as you can see."

Lighthouse George had no patience for Kane's ex-planation. "Wrong," he said. "Very wrong."

"I'm sorry you feel that way." It wasn't really an apology, Nathan realized. He could feel Kane's eyes on him.

Lighthouse George wasn't satisfied. "You show no respect for the dead."

Nathan had never seen George angry before.

"No harm was intended, I assure you." Suddenly the man's blue eyes flickered, and his tone became aggressive. "You shouldn't put those cute little houses on the graves, really. Visitors and newcomers will get the wrong idea."

Nathan was furious that Kane was acting as if the Makahs had entrapped him in some way. He was nothing but a scheming murderer! "What were you looking for?" Nathan blurted, and wished just as quickly he'd held his tongue.

Kane looked right at him, and then at Lighthouse George. Kane's disguises were stripped, or he had cast them aside. There was nothing showing in his blue eyes now but anger and hatred and contempt. "Get out of my way," he snarled, and pushed his way through the gate.

"Stay away from that one," George said as they watched him go.

"I will," Nathan agreed. This time he told himself he meant it.

It was Dolla Bill who suffered the brunt of Kane's wrath. Late in the day, Nathan went to see what finishing touches Young Carver had added to the canoe. Even from a distance he could see that the canoe maker had pegged the prow piece to the body of the canoe. Defying gravity, the prow continued the graceful lift of the canoe and carried it, tapering, far forward of the hull. As Nathan got closer, he heard a man moaning from inside. It was Dolla Bill in his blue jacket with brass buttons. He'd been severely beaten.

Dolla Bill's pocked and tattooed face was a swollen mass of cuts, welts, and abrasions. One eye was swollen shut, his lip was cracked open, and he'd bled from his nose down his neck and onto his jacket. Nathan was moved to pity. He fetched cold, clean water from the creek in a canoe bailer and climbed into the canoe with it. He helped the battered outcast to sit up, and then he poured water on Bill's face. *"Chuck, chuck,"* Dolla Bill moaned, using the Chinook word for "water."

Using his fingers, Nathan tried to wash Dolla Bill's wounds clean and clear his face of dried blood.

"Olo kopa chuck," Dolla Bill pleaded. He was thirsty. Nathan went back to the creek for another bailer full of water. Dolla Bill drank what he could as Nathan spilled water slowly into his mouth.

"Kane?" Nathan whispered.

"Mamook solleks." Dolla Bill's words were thick, strangled.

"You made him mad? How? What did you do?"

Dolla Bill rolled his head around, as if to see if anyone else was nearby. Reassured, he whispered, *"Memaloose illahee."*

"The graveyard? What about the graveyard? Tell me in English, Dolla Bill. No one can hear. What about the graveyard?"

Nathan lifted the canoe bailer, and waited as the beaten man drank a few more swallows.

"Dolla Bill was afraid. Wouldn't go in graveyard. Bad thing, *hyas cultus*," he whispered.

"You wouldn't search the graveyard for him? He had to do it himself?"

Dolla Bill nodded. "Kane mad at Tenas Mac, too."

"He's mad at me? Why?"

Dolla Bill rolled his one eye that remained open. "He knows you have *sla hal* bones."

"I don't have any bones!"

"Why won't you give them?" Dolla Bill whispered

hoarsely. He raised himself and peered over the edge of the canoe.

"He's not around. There's no one here. I told the truth. I don't have any of those bones. They're someone else's."

"Lotsa dollas, Tenas Mac. Kane give lotsa dollas!"

"Those *sla hal* bones are practically worthless if you ask me."

"Not the bones. Inside bone, it tells secret place. Lotsa dollas at that place, must be."

"I don't understand," Nathan said.

Dolla Bill wasn't listening. Suddenly an enormous smile came over the outcast's face, as if he were the happiest man in the world.

"What is it?" Nathan asked. "What do you have to suddenly be so happy about?"

"Dolla Bill knows!" he cackled. "Dolla Bill remembers! Long time ago, when Dolla Bill was a *tenas* man!"

"You remembered something from when you were a child with the Makahs?"

"Place no one will go! Dolla Bill remembers!"

"Remembers what?"

"Things that live in the trees," Dolla Bill answered mysteriously.

He knows, Nathan thought. "Birds?" Nathan asked. "Like birds? Or do you mean birds' nests?"

"Like birds' nests," Dolla Bill agreed with another cackle. "Kane pay lotsa dollas for birds' nests. I say to him, 'No pay, no say!' "

There's no doubt he remembers, Nathan realized. As soon as he tells Kane, they'll search all through the forest, looking for ghost canoes. How many were there? A few, Bim had said. And one of them, up in some tree, will have the bone piece Kane is after. It will take a while, but they'll find it.

"Just because you remembered the thing that Kane wants to know," Nathan said, "that doesn't mean you have to tell him."

"No pay, no say!" Dolla Bill chortled. "Lotsa, lotsa dollas. One hundred dollas!"

"Kane's the one who did this to you! How could you help him?"

Dolla Bill shook his arms and legs, and stretched, then stood up to go.

"You're selling your soul to the Devil!"

"Dolla Bill's soul not worth anything," the outcast replied with a twisted grin. "Dolla Bill, he's only a *cultus siwach*."

"Lighthouse George doesn't think so. Remember, he took you in. He saved your life."

For a few moments, Dolla Bill reflected on what Nathan had said. A peaceful, almost hopeful expression showed through from beneath the battering and disfigurement of his features. In those moments it seemed as if his insanity might be merely a mask he'd created as part of his circus act. Dolla Bill said, quietly and simply, "George waits for me to do right, like him. Then he love me, maybe so. Take me fishing, like you."

"See? That's what I've been saying. Think what that would be like."

"Like you, Tenas Mac?"

"Not like me," Nathan said. "You could live here your whole life, be home. Me, I'll leave here one day."

Dolla Bill touched his hand to Young Carver's beautiful canoe. "Same, same, Tenas Mac!" Dolla Bill stepped over the side of the canoe and started into the darkness.

"Remember what he did to you! You don't have to help him!"

"No pay, no say!"

·19·

Tomorrow Will Be Too Late

The next day, the Makah fishing canoes were bobbing everywhere up and down the Strait. All the fishermen, and every boy old enough to accompany them, were bringing in the salmon to fill the drying racks and the smokehouses.

Nathan and Lighthouse George were trolling for the salmon now. The salmon hooks were simple compared to the bentwood halibut hooks. Spruce-root lashing secured both the bone barb and the leader to a wooden shank. The fishing lines of inner cedar bark, weighted by a sinker stone, were tied to the canoe's thwarts and then held against the shaft of the canoe paddle with the hand closest to the water. With each paddle stroke, the baited hook trailing behind would jump forward as if alive. The abalone-shell lure forward of the hook would twist and flash in the water,

162

providing a reason for the big salmon to come and investigate. That was when they would discover the piece of herring wrapped around the barb of the hook.

The trading post was closed again, for the third consecutive day. Lighthouse George didn't seem very concerned about it. Nathan wished he could explain to George why it was closed. He wanted to tell him that Kane was a treasure-hunter and a murderer, not a trader. He wished George had been able to understand when he'd explained it to him before. But he couldn't say any of these things now. He had to keep it all to himself. Telling would only endanger more people, and Nathan was sure something awful would happen.

The salmon fishing should have been a dream come true, but Nathan couldn't keep his mind on it. He was catching twenty-, thirty-, forty-pound salmon, yet it was as if he wasn't there.

Whenever they found a ghost canoe, he wondered, would they also find bone game pieces? He wished he could ask Lighthouse George. He wished he could quit thinking about Kane and the map he was after, and Kane finding treasure and getting away with murder.

But he couldn't.

On the afternoon of the third day, after they'd come in from fishing, Nathan and George helped Young Carver soak the inside of the canoe with whale oil, to keep the wood from splitting. The canoe maker had added dye to the whale oil, which was turning the inside of the canoe red. Nathan kept looking around to see if he could see Kane and Dolla Bill returning from the forest to the trading post.

He helped scorch the bottom of the canoe with cedar bark torches, to harden the wood. George said they wouldn't go fishing the next day. Young Carver needed some more help with the canoe.

In the morning, on his way to the canoe, Nathan saw people going into the trading post. The store was open again. He knew what that must mean—Kane had found what he was after. The realization made Nathan's temples throb. He felt light-headed and sick in his stomach as well. He made himself walk on by. He couldn't stand to see Kane gloating.

Lighthouse George was sanding the blackened exterior of the canoe with the dried-out skin of a fish. The skin of the dogfish, he said it was. Behind him, where George had sanded, Young Carver was patiently applying oil from a canoe bailer to the canoe's hull with a paintbrush.

Nathan got ready to help with the sanding. He took a sheet of the dogfish skin from the basket under the cedar tree and started sanding with it, down toward the squared-off stern of the canoe. He had a lot to think about. He'd never been so frustrated or so angry in his life.

The next time the *Anna Rose* visited, Kane and Dolla Bill would leave Neah Bay. Kane's sea chests would be extraordinarily heavy. Had they already found the treasure, or merely the map? It was bad enough that Kane had gotten away with murder!

He wanted a glimpse of their faces. He would be so cautious; he just wanted to see if anything could be learned from looking at them. Kane wouldn't be so dangerous now either, not if he already had what he wanted. There was a little money in Nathan's pocket. He only needed a reason for visiting the store.

The dogfish skin in his hand provided the excuse. Real sandpaper would probably work better anyway, he thought.

As Nathan opened the trading post's screen door, Kane's piercing blue eyes were on him. Seated at the table, Kane was lifting a coffee cup to his mouth, and his eyes were staring over the top of the cup. Unnerved, Nathan looked away. Dolla Bill, lying full length on top of the long counter, rolled his eyes in Nathan's direction and said, "Poor Bill is so tired. Poor Bill, so tired."

Nathan told himself not to talk to either of them any more than he had to. He walked directly toward the hardware section at the back of the store and found the sandpaper. He selected the coarsest grade, ten sheets. Young Carver would be happy to have real sandpaper.

Kane glided to the counter to take Nathan's money. Dolla Bill was still lying on his back on the counter, and now he was sighing, "Poor Bill, poor Hundred-Dolla Bill." Nathan saw enough of Kane's eyes to tell him what he wanted to know. Kane wasn't gloating. He was still angry.

Nathan said offhandedly, "They're using fish skin to sand the canoe."

"They are ignorant," Kane replied with a sneer. "What did you expect?"

Kane had completely discarded his mild, warm manner. This was the real Kane.

Nathan knew it would be a mistake to act afraid. He

had to act normal. "Have you been taking a vacation? The store was closed for three days. . . ."

"Precisely," Kane agreed. "Exploring the countryside, while it's nice and dry. Winter comes, we'll be cooped up in here."

"Will the store be open tomorrow, or closed again?"

"I'm still sightseeing. A day's rest might be all I need. Or I might even decide to climb Mount Olympus, and that could take a week or more. Of what concern is all this to you?"

"I guess it's none of my business."

On his way back to George and Young Carver, Nathan thought hard. There were only two possibilities. The first: Kane and Dolla Bill hadn't found the right ghost canoe yet. The second: They had found the right one, and they had the map in their possession. In that case, Kane had already put the two maps together and had determined the location of the treasure, but they were waiting before they actually went after it. Remembering Kane's eyes, he rejected the second possibility. Kane hadn't yet found the *sla hal* piece he was after.

This led Nathan to the thought he'd been trying to push out of his mind ever since he'd read the dead man's letter: What if the *sla hal* piece Kane needed is in the ghost canoe on the mountain above the Cape? What if the map is inside one of the bone pieces he'd once held in his hands? It would be difficult to find that canoe, that was certain—he himself had been lucky to glimpse it from that one angle, through a break in the trees. But wasn't it only a matter of time before Kane and Dolla Bill discovered it?

With both of them in the trading post today, it was his one chance to take the prize away from Kane.

He could throw the bone pieces into the forest, or, better yet, into the sea. Or maybe keep them in a safe place where Kane could never possibly get hold of them. On Tatoosh, with his father. Then he'd be able to explain at last to his father all about the ghost canoe. His father would be amazed that he'd snatched the lost map away from Kane. The other map might be recovered from Kane some other time, maybe by the territorial marshal. . . .

He'd been so deep in thought he hadn't realized he was standing at the side of the canoe, just standing there with the sandpaper in his hand. Young Carver and Lighthouse George were looking at him strangely.

"I got some sandpaper," Nathan explained. "I think it'll work better."

Young Carver was wagging his head. "Tried it," he said with a shrug. "Not as good."

Lighthouse George, who was the one who was sanding, didn't seem inclined either to use the sandpaper. "Well, I'll try it out," Nathan said.

He went back to the spot on the stern where he'd been working. After a few minutes he discovered that Young Carver was right. The sandpaper dulled easily, tore easily. He picked up the piece of dogfish skin again. He had no patience today. The canoe was too big. Anyway, he should be using this day to get back to the ghost canoe. It was his only chance.

It wouldn't be a problem simply to walk away with no explanation; it would be the Makah way. But he couldn't just walk away from Lighthouse George, and there was something he needed to know. It would be

167

too dangerous to keep the map even for a short time, even overnight. He had to know that they could paddle to Tatoosh just as soon as he returned, if he had found it. "I think I'm going to go for a hike," he told Lighthouse George.

"*Klo-she*," Lighthouse George responded, though he seemed a little surprised.

"Will you be here when I get back? Here or at your longhouse?"

"Sure."

"You're not going anywhere in your canoe?"

George shook his head.

"Not going fishing? I wouldn't want to miss any fishing!"

"Tomorrow," George said. "We go again tomorrow."

"*Klo-she*," Nathan agreed.

Confident that they could paddle directly to Tatoosh upon his return, Nathan started up the village creek, and he didn't look back. That would draw attention to himself. He didn't look back until he'd entered the trees. No one was heading his way from the edge of the village. But what if Kane or Dolla Bill had seen him go, and they were just biding their time to catch up with him?

They couldn't have seen me, he thought. They're in the trading post, and Young Carver's canoe can't be seen from the trading post. They think I'm working on the canoe.

Go, he told himself. Now is the time. Tomorrow will be too late. Go!

He soon reached the cedar where Young Carver and Jefferson and the others had been stripping planks on that foggy day in his first weeks at Neah Bay. The freshness of the scar had already dulled. He remembered potlatching his lunch with the silent Makahs, and the strangeness of it all. So much had happened in only a few months. Much of it was still new, but it wasn't so strange anymore.

He started climbing. The climbing caught his breath short. He shouldn't be breathing so loud, he realized. It was midsummer now, and not so easy to walk quietly in the forest. In the rainy season, the forest had absorbed sound, like a sponge. Everything had been so soggy—the great trees, the giant ferns, the salal and berry bushes, the mosses, the mushrooms, the rotting logs, the ground itself.

A small twig cracked underfoot. The dry, brittle sound carried. He stopped and looked around. Nothing.

Nathan waited, beginning to wonder if he might have been followed after all. He couldn't afford to be stepping on twigs, not with Kane.

He scared himself picturing Kane as a mere shadow in the woods. All spring and into summer, Kane had been ghosting around Neah Bay from his cave in the Hole in the Wall or from who knew how many hiding places. Kane was a man who knew his way around the woods, knew how to travel soundlessly in the woods, even at night. And Kane was a killer.

Nathan fought the urge to give up, to go back to sanding the canoe. Stay out of this, he told himself. You know you shouldn't be doing this.

He heard the croaking call of a raven from the steep slope below him. Ravens could speak in so many different voices. For a moment Nathan imagined he'd

·heard a warning call, and it sent a shiver up and down his spine.

Within a heartbeat of his turning back, his desire to thwart Kane overcame his fears. Don't give up, he told himself. You can do this. Be careful. Keep watching.

When he reached the top of the first mountain, he rested. He was trembling, he realized, and not from cold. He couldn't think straight, he knew. If Kane caught him with the map, Kane would kill him. There was no question about that. Then why was he continuing toward the ghost canoe as if he couldn't stop himself?

The raven called again, more urgently than before. He knew that the Makahs held the raven in high regard, but he didn't really know why. All the same, he decided to circle back, to watch the route behind him, and see if he was being followed. Quiet as he might, he came down off the mountain, ducking under giant ferns and crawling the length of a downed giant spruce. Then he contoured his way back to the route he had first taken to the summit, and he waited, crouching in the ferns. Nothing.

He was just about to move when he heard the snap of a twig. Where, he couldn't tell. His heart pounded like a drum; he could barely breathe. He made himself calm down. He waited, five minutes, ten minutes, watching through the ferns. Nothing.

A deer, he told himself. That's all it was. A deer or something else that lives in the woods.

Go home! he told himself. You can't think. You're too scared.

He'd never let his fear get the better of him his

whole life. He resisted it now. Go back to the ghost canoe, he told himself. Find out once and for all, or you'll always regret it. You'll always think you could've stopped Kane, but you were afraid.

Nathan crept his way back up to the first summit. It was almost as if he didn't have a choice anymore. Looking all around, he satisfied himself that he was alone, and he started to breathe easier. Quiet as a cat, he dropped into the saddle between the summits and then picked his way up the second one, more confident now and making not even the slightest sound.

From the second mountain he could see emerald green, fortresslike Tatoosh encircled by its gray cliffs. He could see the lighthouse and all the little white buildings with their red roofs. He could see the surf surging over Jones Rock in the gap between the tip of the Cape and Tatoosh. The image of the square-rigger under full sail appearing there in the fog came suddenly to mind. He imagined the fright of the sailors at finding themselves under the looming walls of Tatoosh. As if he'd been aboard the *Burnaby* himself, he heard the sickening crunch when the ship struck the Chibahdehl Rocks. He saw the sea pouring in on them. . . .

All of a sudden, he realized he didn't even know if he'd been remembering to keep low and walk soundlessly. He'd lost his concentration walking down the slope in the direction of Tatoosh and had gotten slightly off course from the route he'd walked that day when he'd followed the sound of the foghorn toward the sea.

He spun around and looked behind him. Nothing.

He froze. Nothing. Nothing but the swaying and creaking of the giant cedars and the spruces on the windward side of the mountain.

Here was the huge nurse log he'd seen that day: the decomposing cedar with the young cedars all straight in a row growing from the top of the log where they had taken root. A little more to the right . . . a little more to the right, and up . . . He kept looking for a familiar pattern, a jigsaw puzzle pattern to all the shapes of each individual tree and branch that would match the one in his memory.

There, through that gap in the trees, there it was, just as he'd left it. The ghost canoe.

·20·

Too Much Gold

He was so close. There was the ghost canoe, exactly as he'd left it, aloft in the fork of the spruce with its prow pointed toward the sea.

Nathan doubted that Kane and Dolla Bill could have been here—the forest litter on the floor of the clearing surrounding the tree showed not even the slightest trace of disturbance. They might have found other ghost canoes, but they hadn't found this one.

Suddenly he felt completely exposed. His heart was hammering again. He had the eerie sensation that he was being watched from the undergrowth. He couldn't see them, but they could see him. The salal bushes, and the berry bushes, and the fronds of giant ferns were all in motion with the wind. It made him dizzy trying to peer through the foliage to detect a face. He listened for a minute. He could hear nothing but his own heart beating. Still he seemed surrounded by the presence of evil.

Act quickly or leave now!

Nathan glanced above at the moss-covered canoe in the tree. He couldn't bear to leave. This would have been a perfect place, he thought, for the Spanish commander to hold in his memory, so close to the summit nearest the tip of Cape Flattery. If he was right, if he didn't panic, he could keep the map from Kane.

Act quickly!

He found the same small hemlock he had used for a ladder before, and dragged it over to the big spruce. With a grunt, he boosted it up into position and rocked it until it locked against the spruce's lowest branch.

Then he climbed.

When he walked out onto the branch alongside the decaying canoe, he found everything the same: the Makah chief's empty, greenish eye sockets, looking forever toward the sea, his mossy paddle close to his right hand. The coil of rope, the sealing club, and the whaling harpoon Nathan had thought was a spear lay in exactly the positions they had before. The small cedar box was wedged behind the skeleton and under the rudder seat exactly where Nathan had left it.

Carefully, holding his breath, Nathan reached behind the skeleton and grasped the box. He brought it out carefully so as not to touch the bones of the *hyas tyee*. He pried it open as carefully and as quickly as he could.

The *sla hal* pieces were still inside: one banded with black string around its middle, the other unmarked. He could see fine joints on the unmarked one that he hadn't noticed the first time. This time he also noticed that it wasn't as yellowed as the other, not as ancient perhaps. Maybe they weren't a matched pair. Perhaps the Spanish commander had replaced the original unmarked piece with this one.

Nathan slid both of the bone cylinders into his pocket and replaced the cedar box behind the skeleton. He climbed down out of the tree, and he looked around. No one.

He had to know if he was right.

He sat cross-legged at the base of the tree, satisfied himself again that he was alone, then studied the joints on the unmarked bone. With a pull from opposite ends, and a twist, it came open.

A small piece of folded and rolled parchment was sticking out of one of the halves.

Even though he had been looking for such a paper, he was astonished. His heart beat faster still, and he looked around. No one. He unfolded the parchment; it crinkled noisily.

He looked up again, and then his eyes returned quickly to the paper. It was the simplest of maps, not really a map at all. Barely in from the frayed margins of the paper, a large square had been drawn. The four sides of the square had been labeled with the four directions of the compass. Inside the square, in the southwest corner, a small X had been drawn. That was all.

Setting the map down, he fitted the two parts of the bone piece back together and put it into his pocket with the other.

As he was doing so, a quick hand from around the side of the tree snatched the map.

Springing to his feet, Nathan was grabbed from behind. The grasp felt like hoops of iron. "We fool you!" a voice cackled.

His captor's voice was unmistakable. It was Dolla Bill.

A second man appeared from behind the tree. It was Kane, with a smug smile on his face and the map in his hand. "Young MacAllister isn't nearly so clever as he thinks he is," Kane said contemptuously. "Thank you for leading us here. I guessed you would, and I guessed right. You know, we walked within thirty yards of this canoe two days ago and never saw it."

Nathan struggled to get a breath.

"I don't want to have to chase him," Kane snarled at Dolla Bill.

Kane walked away to the far side of the clearing. Taking a second map from inside his jacket, he knelt, oriented the maps one against the other, then held them up so the sun would shine through them. Even from a distance, Nathan could tell that Kane's map was drawn with great detail and appeared to be a map of Cape Flattery's coastline and Tatoosh Island.

Kane laughed a vicious, mocking laugh. "I thank you from the bottom of my heart, MacAllister. X indeed marks the spot."

"Where is all the gold?" Dolla Bill blurted. "Where do we find it?"

"It's been right under our noses the whole time! It's on the Cape itself. Not on Fuca's Pillar, not on Tatoosh. We can get it and leave before anyone knows we're gone."

"Thousand-Dolla Bill!" the outcast cheered.

"I still have a canoe hidden close to here, paddles and all. That fool of a marshal never saw it. No need to go back to Neah Bay for anything. We'll do a disappearing act right from here!"

"How do we get down to the canoe?"

"We'll use the easy route—some old stairs through a crack in the cliffs. MacAllister knows all about them, don't you, MacAllister?"

"I don't know anything," Nathan protested.

With uncanny quickness, Dolla Bill released his bear hug, yet held Nathan by one wrist. His grip was strong as a vise. "What do we do with Tenas Mac?" asked Dolla Bill. "Let's take his shoes, okay? Slow him down."

Nathan began to hope that Kane would let him go. But a sneer appeared on Kane's face, and Nathan knew better.

"You seem to know everything," Kane snarled, "or you wouldn't be here now. You should have accepted my offer of friendship. You made a *grave* mistake, MacAllister."

Soundlessly, another man stepped into the clearing—a Makah. It was Lighthouse George.

"Let Tenas Mac go," George said to Dolla Bill.

Kane folded the small maps calmly, methodically, keeping his eye on George, and put them in an inside pocket of his jacket.

Dolla Bill did as George had asked him to. Nathan went to George's side. "How did you . . . ?"

"Three days now, I can see you have troubles. I saw those two following you."

"We won't say anything," Nathan assured Kane.

Kane laughed.

Lighthouse George looked aloft at the ghost canoe, and back at Kane. "What do you want?"

Nathan said to George, "We don't have to find out what he wants, really. If he just leaves . . ."

Kane said, "MacAllister seems to know exactly what I'm looking for, though he pretends he doesn't."

Kane closed the distance between himself and the other three by half. The sneer was back on his face. He drew a pistol hidden under his broad leather belt and pointed it at George's chest. "Both of them are going to have to die," he said to Dolla Bill.

Nathan knew he had only moments to live. "I'm sorry," he said to Lighthouse George. "This man killed the captain of that ship, the *Burnaby*."

Nathan could see he'd surprised Kane, that he knew even about the murder. Nathan could see understanding begin to come to Lighthouse George's face.

Kane only laughed his contemptuous laugh.

George was taking a long, questioning look at Dolla Bill.

"Dolla Bill hasn't hurt anybody," Nathan explained to George. "Dolla Bill wasn't on that ship. He didn't know Kane back then."

From no more than ten feet away, Kane cocked his pistol and pointed it directly at Lighthouse George's heart. Kane said, "Now that he's had his history lesson . . ."

It was only the briefest impression, but from the corner of his eye Nathan saw a protective look come over Dolla Bill's pocked and bruised face.

Dolla Bill sprang as the gun was fired; it was impossible to tell which had happened first. The outcast lunged with the speed and the agility of an acrobat. His momentum threw Kane to the ground.

It happened too fast for Nathan to tell what had become of the shot he'd heard—only that George didn't seem to have been hit. Dolla Bill tore the pistol from Kane's hand and, with a strangled cry, heaved it far into the underbrush. Then Dolla Bill fell back, and Nathan could see a bullet hole in his chest. The outcast was dead.

Kane glanced in the direction his pistol had been thrown, as he quickly drew out the big knife with the clipper ship design. Then he turned and ran down the mountainside with huge bounding leaps, like an animal.

"He's got a canoe down there," Nathan explained.

"Let him go," George said. "We got lotsa canoes."

Nathan found out how fast the barefoot, stocky Makah could run. Lighthouse George led the way, and they ran like deer all the way to Neah Bay.

Word went around the village in minutes, to the beach, and even offshore, where the fishermen were bringing in the salmon. The Makahs remembered how to go to war. They brought out weapons Nathan didn't even know they had—spears, shields, war clubs made of whalebone, stones the shape of cannonballs for sinking canoes.

Six of the whaling canoes had gone out earlier, when Nathan had joined them on the whale hunt, but eight of them, each crewed by eight men, went out now in pursuit of Kane. It was apparent that the Makahs no longer considered Kane none of their business. He had murdered Dolla Bill, who seemed to have become a Makah at last with the bravery of his final act.

The war canoes rounded Koitlah Point with the paddlers chanting and tapping their paddles on the gunwales between strokes. Through the flying sea spray, Nathan kept his eyes on the channel ahead between the mainland and Tatoosh. With so many men pulling in unison, the streamlined, thin-hulled canoes of lightweight cedar shot through the waters of the Strait around the Chibahdehl Rocks, past the Hole in the Wall and its colonies of screaming seabirds, and around the tip of Cape Flattery.

Kane could have been hiding in any of the Cape's sea caves, but the Makahs sensed he'd be trying to escape down the coast. As the canoes rounded Fuca's Pillar, Nathan hoped to glimpse a lone canoe to the south, but he was disappointed. Kane might be as much as four hours ahead, Nathan realized, depending on how long it had taken him to find the treasure. The gold must have been hidden in a niche in one of the many sea caves around the tip of the Cape. In Kane's haste to get away, had he been able to locate it?

It was going to be a race against the daylight as well as against Kane, Nathan realized. There were only a few hours of light left, maybe three hours including twilight. By cover of night, Kane was sure to escape.

The Makahs loved to race, and their powerful upper bodies supplied them with seemingly endless strength and stamina. Nathan was tiring, but the Makahs showed no sign of tiring. Instead, they were inspired by the chase and continued to skim past the beaches, cliffs, rocks, and reefs of the Cape's southern coast.

The canoes crossed Makah Bay, putting its long spits and beaches behind them, and rounded a head of land to the south of it. Still no canoe came into sight. "What if he's behind us?" Nathan fretted to George, who was behind him with the broad steering paddle.

"Then we get him later."

The canoes kept to the outside of a rock reef, then paddled the length of another long beach toward another point of land with seastacks standing offshore. The sea had carved its way through several of them and shaped them into arches.

By the time the canoes reached the arches, the sea was swallowing the sun. Nathan thought they had lost. George called for more speed, and his paddlers responded, taking the lead from another canoe. George selected a channel through the arches and pointed the canoe toward even more rocks and another head of land a mile to the south.

When they threaded their way through the rocks and rounded the head, a shout went up from the men in the front of the canoe. There he was, barely a half mile ahead of them underneath the tall cliffs: a lone man paddling a single canoe.

In Makah, George called for more speed.

From the war cries that went up behind him, Nathan knew the rest of the canoes were rounding the head now and paddling at full speed.

Kane would have to go to land, that much was certain. If he stayed on the water, the Makahs would catch him.

Kane was paddling as fast as he could. He was trying to reach the beach ahead at the end of the long line of cliffs.

If Kane reached the beach, he could run, use the night, disappear.

Lighthouse George called once more to his paddlers, and they responded. Nathan matched the Makahs stroke for stroke. In another few minutes, as the great canoe kept closing the gap, it became obvious that Kane was not going to be able to get away.

Only a quarter of a mile ahead now, Kane's canoe stopped suddenly. Nathan could make out the murderer leaning forward in the canoe, seizing something. Something extremely heavy, but barely bigger than his hands.

Kane swung and dropped the object over the side. An ingot, Nathan realized. "That's gold," he cried. "Spanish gold!"

George repeated the words in Makah. Word was passed among the canoes; all the Makahs were hushed and watching intently.

Kane reached for a second bar. It went over the side of the canoe, as did a third and a fourth and a fifth. Kane was strong, and he was working as fast as he could.

Under the cliffs and a hundred yards offshore, Nathan knew, it was all deep water, inconceivably deep. If Kane couldn't have the treasure for himself, he was making sure no one else would.

There was nothing to be done. It wasn't possible to get close enough to stop him.

Six, seven, eight, nine, ten, eleven.

The Makahs, having rested for less than a minute, gave a shout and continued the chase. Nathan pulled and pulled with his paddle, his eyes riveted all the while on Kane. Twelve, thirteen, fourteen, fifteen.

The canoes were closing fast on Kane. Now he was paddling directly for shore, where the surging sea was exploding against rocky shelves along the base of the cliffs. Kane was aiming to land the canoe in the only possible break in the tumultuous shoreline, a tiny, sandy cove.

The Makahs, all eight whaling canoes, chased Kane as close to the cliffs as they could. With skillful paddling, Kane succeeded in beaching his canoe in heavy surf. He was hemmed in against the cliffs, but the Makahs weren't inclined to land and to chase him, not if they didn't have to. They didn't want to risk the loss of a single canoe.

The canoes hovered several hundred feet offshore and watched. Nathan saw Kane look back at the Makahs all massed there, then look up at the tall cliff above him, perhaps two hundred feet high. He watched as Kane cut the canoe's bowline loose. He used the line to tie three bars into a bundle—he'd kept three ingots! Kane took off his wide leather belt, secured the gold bars to the belt at its midpoint, then strapped the belt back around his waist.

Kane scrambled away from the cove, along the wave-splashed rocks lining the shore, studying the cliff all the while. Kane was looking for the best route up the cliff. He intended to climb it.

The fugitive chose his spot, and then he began to climb.

Nathan and the Makahs watched Kane pick his way up the cliff, hand over hand, using tiny cracks for handholds. His progress was slow and tedious. He had a long way to go, and the twilight was dimming with every minute. The canoes were too far away for the men to hurl spears or rocks; there was nothing to do but watch.

No one spoke. They watched Kane reach the half-way point. He paused often to rest. It didn't seem humanly possible to do what Kane was doing, but Nathan knew this man had climbed Fuca's Pillar. When he'd climbed the pillar, however, he hadn't had three bars of gold tied at the small of his back. Was he strong enough to overcome the weight of the gold?

Kane was almost to the top. In the murk of approaching darkness, it was difficult to make out the features he was encountering on the cliff. Kane was little more than a shadow now, moving slowly upward. But it appeared he was having to contend with the rock face above him pitching slightly out to sea.

Thirty feet, Nathan guessed. That's all that remained between Kane and his freedom.

Suddenly Kane was struggling. An arm kept grasping for a hold, and his entire body seemed to be leaning farther and farther away from the cliff. His center of gravity, Nathan realized, had shifted to the gold at the small of his back.

What now? Nathan thought. What's he going to do now? How can he be strong enough to hold on?

He wasn't.

One moment Kane was still clinging to the cliff, and the next he was falling backward, face up, plummeting to the rocks below.

Kane never cried out. He had those few seconds left as he was falling, and then he disappeared among the jumble of rocks below the cliff.

Nathan stood up in the canoe, trying to catch a

glimpse of Kane's body. Would he have been killed instantly?

Then he saw him, utterly motionless, heaped on a boulder with his head, arms, and legs askew, like a rag doll twisted limb from limb.

It had ended so quickly. Nathan was unable to believe what he'd just seen. He closed his eyes, steadying himself against the side of the canoe. He knew he shouldn't feel sorry for Kane. This was a cruel, evil man, without pity or remorse, who would have taken Nathan's life and George's too. Yet Nathan hadn't been ready to see this. He felt exhausted, overwhelmed.

"We can go home now," Lighthouse George said gently, his hand on Nathan's arm.

"He almost got away," Nathan said as he sat back down.

George nodded. "Too much gold."

·21·
Everything Passes, Everything Changes

July turned to August. The drying racks all over Neah Bay and across the roofs of the longhouses reflected the Makahs' great wealth—the teeming abundance of the sea. The village smelled of fish and burning alder smoke from all the smokehouses, and was filled with the sound of screaming seagulls from dawn until dark. The sun had bleached the gigantic skeleton of the gray whale a bright white.

Nathan started going barefoot like the Makahs. His feet grew as tough and calloused as Lighthouse George's, and his hands as rough. Paddling the canoe was second nature to him now, as familiar as the scent of cedar.

Every day he felt himself getting stronger, and he relished all the fishing with Lighthouse George. He knew it wouldn't last. Each day was shorter than the

186

one before, each night a little longer and a little colder.

While the sea air was making him grow stronger, it was having the opposite effect on his mother. Summer was almost gone, and his mother's health still hadn't improved. To Nathan and his father, she seemed weaker than she had in April, when she'd first moved from Tatoosh to Neah Bay. The Indian agent finally announced the long-postponed visit of the doctor from Port Townsend. In the last week of August he arrived at last to spend a week tending to the people of Neah Bay. Nathan and Lighthouse George paddled out to Tatoosh to bring his father to Neah Bay to hear what the doctor would say about his mother's health.

Nathan's mother was examined at the Indian Agency. Nathan and his father were called into the doctor's temporary office after the examination was completed so they could all hear the results together. The doctor's expression was solemn. Nathan had the panicky feeling that his mother was mortally sick.

"I regret that I am about to frighten you," the doctor began, looking over his reading glasses. He was an old man, thin and bald. Nathan's mother was trying to quell her cough as the doctor spoke, but she couldn't.

Nathan felt himself being overcome by grief, as if he'd already lost her.

"I am too old and have seen too much to be indirect," the doctor continued. "Tuberculosis is on the rise again in every little town up and down the coast. Mrs. MacAllister has been sick for some time now, and in her weakened condition, she will contract it soon, in my judgment. With the turn of the weather and the advent of the fall storms—"

"What you are saying, Doctor," Nathan's father interrupted, "is that Mrs. MacAllister does *not* have tuberculosis?"

"That's correct. But I would say she is highly disposed toward it."

"Thank God. It was my worst fear. Then she can still get well—she can recover fully?"

"That's correct," replied the doctor. "But her illness is serious, make no mistake. She must leave this climate, in my opinion."

"We will, then," Captain MacAllister said without hesitation, his large hand reaching for his wife's shoulder.

The doctor nodded approvingly. "That would be my advice, and soon."

Nathan's mother objected, "You can't give up the sea, Zachary."

"It's time," his father said. "It's just as well. I'm weary of the confinement that comes with the lighthouse life. It's like being on a ship that never arrives in port."

That evening back in the cottage, Nathan's parents talked of the warm valley of California, where his mother had been raised, and they talked of a farm, and orchards, and cattle. His father thought they had enough savings to buy a very small farm, and if they were successful after some years, it would become a ranch. He could see his mother's habitual determination being rekindled as they spoke.

Nathan listened carefully. He willed himself to picture the farm and the fruit trees and maybe a horse for him.

It was a good picture, but it lacked the sea. Salt water was in his veins. His heart was full of the surging Pacific and the screaming gulls and the fragrance of cedars. He would even miss the power of the winter storms. But he would miss Lighthouse George most of all.

He said none of these things. He thought about the vision of the farm. They would have their own land; they would make it productive. His mother had spoken occasionally over the years of the beauty and fertility of the great valley of California, watered by mountain rivers on their way to the ocean. In the heat of California, his mother could grow all the flowers and vegetables she ever wanted. In the heat of the valley, she would regain her health.

His parents paused, waiting for his reaction. He knew his mind. More than anything, it was important that he pull his share. "I want to help build that farm," he said decisively.

"You make me proud," his father said.

"When will we go?"

"We'll not wait for the Lighthouse Service to replace me. That will take until spring, unless they are forced to act by my absence. I'll let them know immediately that I'm leaving. Then they'll find another head keeper in a month. Perhaps one of the assistants might even be suitable."

"The valley of California . . . ," Nathan's mother repeated. Spoken from her lips, it was a hopeful and magical phrase.

She turned to her only child and studied his face. "Are you just being brave about leaving, Nathan?

What do you really feel? You'll miss the sea, I know. We all will. You'll miss Neah Bay. And I fear you will miss Lighthouse George terribly."

He knew how hard it was going to be for him to leave. But he found his answer in something his mother had once told him, a saying he now repeated back to her: "Everything passes, everything changes."

And it was true. His time at Neah Bay seemed to have passed like fog blowing out to sea. It hadn't become his home, yet the people and the place had become a part of him, a part that he would keep with him wherever he went.

Perhaps he'd return, one day. Return and visit Lighthouse George.

Two more weeks were all that remained, the first two weeks of September. Two weeks of fishing with George during the last salmon run of the season. The silvers were running in abundance; the drying racks and the smokehouses were once again full. During this interval Captain Bim returned to reopen the trading post, surprising no one more than himself by how much he had missed Neah Bay. He was happy simply to be back, happier still when he discovered the place where Kane had hidden the remainder of his twenty-dollar gold pieces.

Young Carver finished the new whaling canoe, and Nathan helped to launch it and paddle it out into the bay and around Waadah Island.

On the day before they were to leave on the *Anna Rose,* Nathan's mother baked a birthday cake for his father. His father's fifty-second birthday was still a week away, but they would be on a steamer heading south then, and among strangers. His mother invited Lighthouse George and Rebecca to be their guests for their last evening in Neah Bay.

George brought several fresh silver salmon, which Rebecca roasted the Makah way, upright on small frames of cedar sticks, by a small campfire outside the cottage. Nathan's father and mother told George and Rebecca that they'd never tasted such delicious salmon, which brought a smile to Rebecca's face. After supper, as the sun was setting, Nathan went inside to bring out the cake, which his mother had hidden in the cupboard.

Nathan disregarded the birthday candles his mother had set out. He had a surprise for his father, the sort of birthday gesture that would strike his fancy. Earlier in the day, Nathan had gone to the longhouse for half a dozen dried eulachon. He'd been wanting to perform this experiment for weeks and had never gotten the chance. His father's birthday provided the perfect opportunity.

He stuck the small smeltlike fish into the cake, heads first. Then he lit the tails of "the fish that burns," and was delighted with the outcome. Every tail was burning brightly as he stepped outside and presented the cake to his father.

His father, for a certainty, had never seen such a sight. Barely able to contain his laughter, he managed to blow out the burning tails.

The evening held another surprise, this one from Lighthouse George. After they finished eating their cake, George reached under a piece of cloth in Rebecca's basket and brought out something wrapped in an embroidered piece of linen. Nathan guessed it was a loaf of bread, a gift for his father. Instead, George handed it to Nathan, who wasn't prepared for its improbable weight. A bar of solid gold fell to the ground.

One of the ingots that had been on Kane's body, Nathan realized immediately.

"It's for the new farm," George said proudly. "Lotsa land."

Nathan's father was speechless.

"The Makahs only have three bars," his mother said to Nathan.

"I know," Nathan replied, looking at his fishing partner. "You want us to have one?"

Both George and Rebecca nodded, and Nathan knew he couldn't refuse this gift. His parents knew it, too.

"Thank you," Nathan said.

Lighthouse George shrugged. "We give away the others sometime, too. Big potlatch."

The next day, Nathan and George paddled out to the *Anna Rose*. As they neared the steamer, Nathan knew the last of his time in the canoe was running out, his time with George. His family's household goods and their trunks of clothing, ferried out to the steamer on platforms of cedar planks spanning two canoes, had already been loaded aboard the ship. His parents had gone ahead as well, after saying their good-byes in the village.

It was time for Nathan to climb out of the canoe. At first he couldn't find words to say to George. All he had was feelings, far too deep for words. Then he said, "Thank you," and he took his paddle out of the water and rested it inside the canoe, against the thwart. His eyes went misty, and he said, "Good-bye, George."

"Keep that paddle, *Yaw-ka-duke,* to remember me. You're a good puller, good fisherman, good friend."

"I don't have anything to leave with you."

George smiled and tapped his heart.

"I'll come back one day. I know I will."

George nodded. "I'll save a place in the canoe for you."

Nathan stepped out of the canoe with his paddle. He didn't look back until after he'd disappeared inside and climbed to the ship's upper deck, where he joined his parents.

The *Anna Rose* sounded its horn, reminding Nathan of the great fog trumpet on Tatoosh.

George paddled his graceful canoe safely clear of the ship, and then he spun it around and watched the huge steamer pull out, spouting dense black smoke from its stacks.

Nathan kept his eyes fixed on Lighthouse George and his canoe. Within minutes the man and the canoe were melding together and blurring in the distance. Neah Bay's longhouses, behind, were blending into the forest. Nathan lifted his paddle high and waved it three times in the air.

He was able to make out a paddle waved three times in reply.

Author's Note

While *Ghost Canoe* is a work of fiction, it is grounded in the geography, natural history, and human history of the Northwest. The Cape Flattery Lighthouse on Tatoosh Island had indeed seen a succession of bachelor lighthouse keepers since its light first shone on December 28, 1857. In 1874, the year of my story, plans were in the offing to improve the living quarters in order to attract a keeper with a family. Although the light itself was automated in 1977, the original lighthouse still stands on Tatoosh today.

Mail was delivered from Neah Bay to Tatoosh Island during the 1870s by dugout canoe. Lighthouse Jack was the mailman's name, and Young Doctor was the name of a prominent canoe carver of the era. I have named my fictional characters Lighthouse

George and Young Carver as a tribute to these actual historical figures.

The Chinook trading jargon, drawn from a number of native languages, as well as French and English, was at the height of its usefulness and popularity in the 1870s, spoken by at least a hundred thousand people in the Northwest. Vestiges of the Chinook jargon can still be found in place-names and regionalisms today. A few Chinook words found their way into broader modern English, as in the expression "high-muck-a-muck," thought to have originally described chiefs with much food to give away at potlatches.

Ghost Canoe was inspired by the canoes themselves. The great canoes are once again being carved from Western red cedar trees by native people, including the contemporary Makah, from Washington State up through British Columbia to southeast Alaska, and paddled on the waters of the Pacific. They are a sight to see.